The Mystery of the
Hooded Horseman

The Mystery of the Hooded Horseman

Mysteries in Odyssey

John Beebee

Tommy nelson™
A Division of Thomas Nelson, Inc.
www.tommynelson.com
www.ThomasNelson.com

Published in Nashville, Tennessee, by Tommy Nelson, a division of Thomas Nelson, Inc. Scripture quotations are from THE HOLY BIBLE: NEW INTERNATIONAL VERSION. Copyright © 1973, 1978, 1984 by International Bible Society. Used by permission of Zondervan Publishing House. All rights reserved.

This is a work of fiction, and any resemblance between the characters in this book and real persons is coincidental.

Library of Congress Cataloging-in-Publication is Available

ISBN 1-561799-73-4

Printed in the United States of America

02 03 04 05 06 PHX 5 4 3 2 1

Prologue

Darkness enveloped him. The only light in the room was from the computer monitor. He looked over his shoulder. The blue-white glow of the computer screen created strange shadows around him, including a misty shadow of himself, hovering near the ceiling.

He glanced out the window beside him. The streetlight cast a puddle of pale yellow on the curb below. And out of the night, a gray sports car appeared, slowly circling the building like a shark. He bit his lip. The clock at the bottom of his monitor read 7:52.

His brown fingers were now a blur as they flew feverishly across the keys. Each key obeyed his touch, his fingers making a music all their own. His palms grew moist.

Thirty minutes ago, these same hands had held one of the most precious possessions in the world—a dark cherry-brown violin. Three hundred thirty-eight years old. Appraised at $2.7 million. Yesterday, the city of Chicago and the Chicago Museum of Music and Culture had launched a full-scale investigation—

dispatching members of a secret security force around the world to recover the stolen instrument. But no one could have known it was now tucked safely away inside an old Victorian mansion, in a quaint little town called Odyssey.

He felt a chill across his neck. He looked back at the window behind him. The curtains floated gently on the breath of a night breeze. He squinted at the dimly lit white board on the wall, where someone had scrawled a message:

This Week's Verse: 1 Samuel 16:7
Don't forget Kids' Radio Meeting Tonight!

Suddenly, a black leather glove covered the man's face. He writhed and twisted to get free. There was a hissing sound—a strong, sweet smell—a nauseating dizziness. He dropped to the floor. The last thing he felt was a skinny rope winding quickly around his wrists. Then *black*.

NAME: Jared DeWhite
CODE NAME: Agent 3XQ
MISSION: Locate and apprehend El Garbanzo, hiding somewhere in the building, before he escapes with the infamous Z-Gun—the most powerful weapon of destruction ever seen on the planet.

I n the dark hallway, a lanky twelve year old wearing a blue baseball cap and skateboarding T-shirt quietly slid along the wall—police-style. The boy, known as "Agent 3XQ," sensed that someone was nearby. Very nearby. His eyes pierced through the shadows like a laser, his ears tuned in the slightest movement like a radar dish, his nose picked up the faintest aroma like a smoke detector with a brand new battery.

1

Nothing to fear. He had the only weapon he needed— his brilliant mind.

Suddenly, a figure stepped out in front of him. For Agent 3XQ, there was only one logical response . . . "AAAAAAAAAAAAAAH!"

3XQ rarely used his powerful secret agent lungs in this manner. But a spy must always be on the alert—ready to employ his life-saving skills at a moment's notice.

Only the figure that emerged from the shadows wasn't El Garbanzo. It was Mr. Whittaker.

He stood directly under a ceiling light, which made his white hair glow. The tall and broad inventor looked down at Jared through his round spectacles—a curious look in his eye. There was a hint of a smile under his bushy mustache.

"Jared, are you all right?"

"Um, sure," Jared stammered. "Yes. I'm just fine. Thank you."

Boy, was that *embarrassing,* Jared thought. *Training to be a secret agent is tough enough without being* discovered—*the Ultimate Booboo in secret agenting.*

This mission had started off as a simple trip to the restroom. Jared had quickly recognized the chance to turn this restroom trip into a training exercise. But now that exercise had gone awry. *I might as well have "I AM A TOP SECRET AGENT" printed across my baseball cap,* Jared thought.

"Let's head back to Kids' Radio," Mr. Whittaker said. "Sarah's probably ready to go home."

"All right," said Jared.

As he walked with Mr. Whittaker down the long hallway, Jared remembered something Sarah had said a while back. There was a rumor that Mr. Whittaker had actually been a real-life spy himself at one time. Jared wasn't sure if the rumor was true. He wanted to ask Mr. Whittaker about it, but *how?* You couldn't just run up to somebody and say, "Excuse me, are you or have you ever been a spy for the United States government?" You had to wait for the right moment for these kinds of things. Besides, he didn't want to blow Mr. Whittaker's cover.

As a budding secret agent himself, Jared duly noted his environment. Usually, this place was teeming with kids everywhere. After all, Whit's End was the ultimate kids' hangout. You could create your own radio show in the Kids' Radio Studio, hide in the belly of a big fish in the Jonah display, or enter the "Room of Consequence," where your imagination could take you into the future. You'd find kids slurping malts at the Soda Shop, exploring the Bible Room upstairs, or re-creating historic train wrecks in the Train Room.

But now, in the silent shadows of the old mansion, the only kids there were Jared DeWhite and Sarah Prachett.

Yep, after closing time, Whit's End was strangely quiet. And so was Mr. Whittaker, come to think of it. The little smile Jared caught earlier was gone now. What was going on?

As the founder of Whit's End, Mr. Whittaker was always around, ready to stir up a new adventure. He liked to chat about his latest invention or discuss Jared's latest conspiracy theory. But tonight, Mr. Whittaker's gaze was fixed straight ahead. As if he was thinking about something.

"Are you okay, Mr. Whittaker?" Jared asked.

"Oh. I'm sorry, Jared," he said. "I've just got a lot on my mind." Jared thought he heard a quiet sigh.

"Is there any way I can help?" Jared asked. It felt weird. Usually, Mr. Whittaker was the one who offered a listening ear. He was sure Mr. Whittaker would reply with something vague like, "Oh, it's nothing to worry about." But to Jared's surprise, Mr. Whittaker confided in him.

"I just got word today that an old friend of mine has disappeared," said Mr. Whittaker. "And there's speculation . . . he might have died."

Whoa. Heavy stuff, Jared thought. He didn't want to ask any more questions. Not because he wasn't curious, of course. Jared was *always* curious. But it seemed like it would be rude to pry into Mr. Whittaker's personal life. All he could think to say was, "Oh."

Maybe this incident has something to do with Mr. Whittaker's spy days, Jared couldn't help thinking. *His spy buddy was probably ambushed in a hostile country.*

Mr. Whittaker swung open the bright green door labeled "Kids' Radio" and motioned for Jared to go in first. It was a good-sized studio, with about five or six microphones mounted on shiny chrome stands and gathered in a corner of the room. Black metal music stands—which the actors used to hold their radio scripts—stood at attention against the wall. Wires were arranged all over the floor like neatly organized spaghetti.

Sarah sat on one of the gray stools scattered around the studio, a yellow legal pad in her lap. She was copying down ideas from the board on the wall, which was covered with words written in green, blue, and red marker.

> 1 A flower—named Daisy Mae—is very sad. The flowers around her think she is really ugly.

Jared didn't want to read anymore. It was totally ridiculous.

Sarah, a miniature but feisty eleven year old, brushed back some of her short strawberry blonde hair and put it behind her ear. Her freckled face hovered over the yellow pad as she continued to write.

"So, how do you two think it went tonight?" Mr. Whittaker asked.

Sarah jumped in before Jared even opened his mouth—as usual. "I think it went great!" she said in her slightly raspy voice, without even looking up.

"Yeah," Jared echoed halfheartedly. *For* YOU, he thought. He picked up his own yellow pad from one of the gray stools.

At the top of the pad were tiny letters scrawled in number two pencil:

5

Man looks at the outward appearance, but the Lord looks at the heart. 1 Samuel 16:7

Earlier that night, Mr. Whittaker's Sunday school class had gathered in the Kids' Radio Studio to come up with ideas for a Kids' Radio show, using this verse. Jared was sure *his* radio show idea was divinely inspired. It had all started off with a brilliant concept. Then a colossal idea hit him—WHAM!—and pretty soon, it snowballed into an epic movie script with blockbuster special effects and super movie stars.

Jared was sure that a hundred years from now, this very pad full of notes would wind up under glass at the Smithsonian Institution, in the Jared DeWhite Wing. A bronze plaque beside the yellow pad would say: "This is where Jared DeWhite's worldwide fame all began. Little did anyone know what a powerful impact the amazing DeWhite would make upon the fair citizens of earth with his movies, his books, and his commercial endorsements."

But for now, he'd have to keep his prized yellow pad in safekeeping. His idea—about three-eyed space aliens coming to earth disguised as discount shoe salesmen—had been rejected by Sarah and the entire Sunday school class.

So what did *they* know?

Instead, the class went with Sarah's idea. It was something about a little flower that's so awfully ugly, no bee would come near it. Sarah said her idea would make a "pithy" radio drama. Jared wasn't sure what "pithy" meant—probably something like "pitiful."

That was another thing that annoyed Jared. Sarah was always pushing her way around. And the class seemed to always side with *her*. It hurt a bit. After all, Jared's ideas were original, unique, unusual. Okay, and a little bizarre. But nobody appreciated his creativity. Instead, the class seemed to like the safe, "tried-and-true" ideas. Like a flower and a bee. Yawn.

Jared slipped the pad into his backpack.

"I'm done now," Sarah said as she put her pen on the tray of the white board.

"Good," said Mr. Whittaker. "Time to take you two home."

Jared and Sarah lived next door to each other, and Mr. Whittaker had offered to give them a ride home.

"Just have to lock up the place and we'll be on our way," Mr. Whittaker said.

Hmm, lock up the place . . . Jared's spy-brain shifted into gear. This rambling, historic mansion fascinated him, and he'd always had a curious hunger to discover all the secret rooms and hidden passageways he'd heard about.

He remembered the time when Nick—who worked part-time at Whit's End in the Soda Shop—gave him a "behind the scenes" tour. Nick seemed to like showing off what he knew about things. It was a slow day at the Soda Shop, so they headed up the spiral staircase . . .

A dusty old pump organ sat in the corner of the attic. Nick claimed that if you played certain notes on the organ, some panels in the wall would open up to another room. Nick had forgotten the tune, though. It was some song about a cabbage.

Next, they headed downstairs to the basement, where Nick pointed out a huge cabinet. Behind that cabinet, he said, was a door that led to the legendary "Secret Room." But he wasn't about to *open* the door. No way. Rumor had it that Mr. Whittaker had found a skeleton in there one time.

Before they left the basement, Nick showed Jared the most amazing part of all—something only a few people knew about. It was an underground tunnel built by a pastor named Reverend Andrew during the Civil War. Reverend Andrew had lived in a rectory above the tunnel, on the site of what was now Whit's End. He used the secret passageway to hide runaway slaves and then help them escape to freedom in the North.

"Can I help you lock up the place, Mr. Whittaker?" Jared suddenly offered. *Another chance to explore!* Jared thought.

"Thank you, Jared," Mr. Whittaker said. "Could you please turn off the lights and lock the Bible Room door upstairs?" *Rats,* Jared thought with a sigh. *No secret panels or skeletons or underground passageways this time. Oh, well.*

"Sure," Jared replied as politely as he could. Mr. Whittaker handed him the keys. Jared knew the routine. After all, he had helped lock up the Bible Room last week. It needed extra security because the Imagination Station was inside. If anyone happened to break into Whit's End—which had happened once before—Mr. Whittaker didn't want anyone getting near his most popular invention.

Sarah followed Jared up the stairs. *As if I need help turning off the lights! Ha!* Jared thought. He knew the truth. There was only one person as curious about this place as he was. And she was just two steps behind him.

Jared could hear Mr. Whittaker clicking off light switches downstairs. Sarah didn't say anything as they climbed the wooden stairway. It was dark except for the green glow of an EXIT sign in the hallway above them.

The third stair from the top creaked under his weight. The sound sent a chill down his back. He didn't know why. Then he stopped cold.

"What are you doing?" asked Sarah.

"Um, nothing." Jared gulped, staring ahead. As he watched, the door to the Bible Room slammed shut all by itself! BANG!

"Did you do that?" Sarah asked.

"No. How could I?" Jared answered.

Jared loudly jingled the keys in his hand, just to let

whoever—or whatever—was on the other side of the door know that someone was coming. The jingling made him feel a little braver for his mission.

"Jared?"

"WHAT?!"

Jared didn't really mean to yell. It was just that Sarah startled him.

"Never mind," said Sarah.

Just a few more steps . . . Jared told himself, hoping his body would start working again soon. But his legs felt like two spaghetti noodles.

"Are you okay?" asked Sarah.

"Yes!" Jared whispered back, trying to reassure himself.

He loudly cleared his throat. He stepped forward. He jingled the keys. Then he reached down to turn the shiny black metal doorknob. The door slowly squeaked open . . .

S arah thought Jared was acting a bit weird. Then again, weird was pretty normal for Jared. But why was he taking so long to open the door? Jared acted as if he half expected an orange polka-dotted monster to peek around the corner, stick out its tongue, and say "Boo!"

Jared can't really be scared because the door shut by itself, can he? It was probably just caused by the wind blowing through an open window or something like that. *That Jared. Always suspicious about everything.*

"I can't find it!" Jared whispered. She heard his hand pawing frantically up and down the inside wall of the room. "It's . . . it's *gone!*"

"What's gone?" Sarah asked.

"The light switch! It . . . disappeared!"

"Jared?"

11

"Yeah?"

"It's on the *other* side of the door."

"Oh," said Jared quietly, "I, uh, kinda forgot about that."

True, it didn't make sense for the switch to be there. Mr. Whittaker had said so. During a recent remodeling of the Bible Room, the electrician accidentally put the light switch behind the door, instead of next to it.

"Do you want me to get the light?" Sarah offered.

"No," Jared whispered. "I can handle it."

Sarah wondered if Jared *could* handle a light switch all by himself.

CLICK!

The switch turned on the overhead lights, and the displays around the Bible Room came alive. Maps that looked like they were printed on ancient parchment hung on the walls. Directly ahead was the David and Goliath display. The mannequins were so lifelike that Sarah always had to remind herself that they weren't actually real. Goliath's head touched the ceiling. Sarah never did like to look at the big guy directly. His deep-set black eyes looked too evil for her.

Next to that was a miniature, true-to-scale ark from the story of Noah, and a nine-foot replica of the Tower of Babel. On the wall beside the tower was the Talking Mirror, which would light up whenever you quoted a Bible verse nearby. Next to the mirror was a gray metal door with a window, which led into the Control Room for the Imagination Station. The white board was posted nearby, and someone had scribbled a few words on it:

This Week's Verse: 1 Samuel 16:7
Don't forget Kids' Radio Meeting Tonight!

Then—something caught Sarah's eye. The window. The curtains were gently moving in the moonlight. *Aha!* Sarah thought.

"There you go, Jared," she said.

"What?"

"This is why the door shut by itself." Sarah crossed the room to close the window. "See?"

"I figured it was something like that," Jared said.

"Oh, *sure!*"

Still, Sarah had to admit something didn't seem right. It was fall—and autumn nights in Odyssey were chilly. It didn't make sense for Mr. Whittaker to have the window open. Sarah peered outside into the darkness. She glanced down to the roof that jutted out just below. Nothing *seemed* unusual. With a grunt, she yanked the wooden frame and slammed the window shut.

"Sarah?" Jared's voice sounded a little uneasy.

"Yes?"

Sarah turned around to see Jared staring at the Imagination Station. To anybody else, everything would have *appeared* normal. The machine, which looked something like a two-seater helicopter cockpit attached to the front of a refrigerator truck, took up a good part of the room. Usually Mr. Whittaker would sit at the control console—a display of gadgets and dials with a keyboard and computer screen—and program the adventure.

Once inside the machine, you'd experience all the sights, sounds, and sensations of actually taking part in some event from history—such as the birth of Jesus, or the Battle of Lexington, or Thomas Edison's invention of the light bulb. The whole thing looked and sounded and smelled *real,* and it would feel like you were spending days in the adventure. Actually, it would all take place in your imagination, and in real time, would only last about fifteen minutes.

But Sarah could see why Jared was alarmed. Something wasn't right here. One of the doors on the Imagination Station was open. She knew that Mr. Whittaker always kept the doors shut for safety reasons. He was the only one allowed to open the Imagination Station when it was time for a new adventure.

Sarah looked over at Jared. *Oh no.* She recognized that wild look in his eye. Whenever Jared's eyes sparkled, it usually signaled the birth of one his wild "theories." This time it was probably something to do with space aliens with removable face plates, or a government conspiracy to release well-trained armies of genetically altered killer turkeys, or hidden spy cameras cleverly disguised as cans of Spaghetti Doodly-O's.

Jared blurted out, "Some evil corporate competitor of Mr. Whittaker's has come to kidnap the Imagination Station and hold it as ransom until Mr. Whittaker coughs up the secret recipe for his Raspberry Ripple ice cream!"

Sarah rolled her eyes with a sigh. "Oh, brother." Jared never met a conspiracy he didn't like. And if he didn't meet one, he'd make one up.

"I'm not sure if I'm going to survive the ride home," she quipped. Just then, Sarah heard the stairway squeak in the hallway behind them. They both froze, silent.

The door yawned open . . .

"What's going on?" Mr. Whittaker said as he walked in.

Sarah let out a sigh of relief. Jared almost fainted. Not that he would have admitted it, of course.

"The window was open," Sarah explained.

"And so was the door to the Imagination Station," Jared chimed in as soon as he found his voice.

"Oh, really?" said Mr. Whittaker.

He walked over to the Imagination Station and glanced at the console beside it. "Well, this is strange," he said, scratching his chin with his thumb. "I know I turned this off earlier." He peeked inside the open door of his invention. "Hmmm."

Mr. Whittaker stepped in and sat down in the leather seat. A solid panel separated him from the other side of the cockpit. Jared heard something click. The automatic door hissed as it slid forward and covered Mr. Whittaker. His voice came over the tinny intercom speaker. "I won't be long."

Jared jumped over to the control panel and pressed the blue intercom button.

"Roger. Ten-four. Over and out."

He'd always wanted to say that.

Sarah rolled her eyes. "Boys!"

"Whaddya mean, *'boys'?"* said Jared.

"Never mind," said Sarah. "You wouldn't understand. After all you *are* one."

"What's *that* supposed to mean?"

"It's a matter of maturity," Sarah continued. "Boys mature much slower than girls, which is why girls are generally smarter and more emotionally advanced than boys."

"Oh, yeah?" Jared said. He wished he could come up with a more mature response. After all, Sarah had just insulted his entire gender, and it was up to him to defend boys everywhere.

"Well . . ." he said. "Well, well, well." *Hmmm. This is a good stalling tactic. The ol' "well, well, well" routine.* "I'd like to *see* where you read *that* information," Jared countered. *Oh, yeah. That was good. Got her on the defensive now.*

"It's been proven by years of research and is a widely accepted scientific fact," Sarah responded smugly.

"Well, *I* don't widely accept it."

They went back and forth like a ping-pong match until Sarah finally interrupted. "What's Mr. Whittaker *doing?*" she asked.

"I have no idea," said Jared. He looked at his watch. Something wasn't right.

"How long has it been?" asked Sarah.

"About ten minutes, I think," answered Jared.

"I think you need to check in on him, just to make sure he's okay."

Jared pressed the intercom button.

"Mr. Whittaker?"

He paused, waiting for an answer.

"Mr. Whittaker?"

No response.

Sarah knocked on the door.

Nothing.

She rapped harder. Still nothing.

She grabbed the door handle. Locked.

Jared hit the button labeled "DOOR LOCK—LEFT" on the control console. Nothing happened. He pressed again and again. Sarah circled around beside him.

"What about that one?" Sarah said, pointing to the next button labeled "DOOR LOCK—RIGHT." Jared pressed it. There was a hiss. "C'mon!" Sarah called and dashed to the far door of the Imagination Station.

Sarah had already climbed in by the time Jared got there. There was only one seat, but it was just wide enough for him to squeeze in beside Sarah.

While Sarah looked at the controls on the dash, Jared reached over her and pounded on the panel separating the two sides of the cockpit. "Mr. Whittaker?" he called out. "Mr. Whittaker!"

"Jared, look out!" Sarah cried.

The door hissed and started to close.

Jared pulled his foot inside—and just in time. As the door latched in place, the last bit of light from outside turned into a tiny sliver and disappeared. Darkness enveloped Jared and Sarah. Jared had been on quite a few adventures, but he didn't remember it ever being so dark.

"I don't like this," said Sarah. "I've got a thing about being in tight spaces . . . especially in the dark."

He tried to think of something brave to say, but all that came out was, "Um . . ."

Wow. Real brave there, Jared.

Suddenly, the dash lit up in front of them.

"Hurry! Buckle the seat belt!" Jared yelled. He knew what was about to happen.

"What?" Sarah was confused.

"The Imagination Station. It's starting by itself!" Jared cried.

Jared now realized why Sarah couldn't reach the seat belt. It was on *his* side.

The machine began to vibrate as a whirling, whining sound rose in pitch and volume around them. He felt around for the metal latch of the seat belt. *Found it!* He pulled it straight up and yanked it as far as it would go, then swung it over to Sarah's side to latch both of them in.

"Buckle it, Sarah!" he yelled over the machine's escalating din.

Sarah grabbed the buckle and latched it.

Electronic, pulsing sounds swirled around them as the Imagination Station shook more and more violently. A yellow light on the dash started flashing. The cockpit glowed yellow—on and off, on and off. The floorboards rattled under their feet.

Suddenly, Jared felt as if they had been dropped from the top of a tall building. His stomach came up in his throat as they plunged in a free fall. It was like they were riding an out-of-control, spiraling roller coaster. Diving, diving, diving.

"WHOOOOAAAAAAH!" Jared yelled. With an upward jerk, the diving feeling leveled off. A sudden lurch, and it felt as if they were in some kind of rocket car hurtling forward. Powerful G-forces slammed them against the seat. Jared inhaled. From the corner of his eye, he saw Sarah's face flash yellow. She took a deep breath and closed her eyes tightly.

The blinking yellow light on the dash was now joined by an alternating green light. Yellow, green, yellow, green. The cockpit pulsated with light and rattled with a rhythmic clatter.

And then, with a jolt, the whirring whine of the Imagination Station slowed in pitch and volume, like a jet engine shutting down. The door lock made a popping sound like a gunshot. Sarah jumped at the sudden noise.

With a hiss, the door slowly slid open, and a cool breeze hit Jared's side.

He could breathe again. He sat in his seat until his mind and body stopped spinning. Then he looked out the door into darkness. Stars were overhead.

"Where are we?" Sarah asked. She unbuckled the seat belt.

"I don't know," said Jared. "Why don't we stay inside, where it's safe?" Jared asked.

"You call this machine *safe?* C'mon, let's take a look around."

Jared and Sarah stepped outside into the night. Jared looked behind them. Instead of the Imagination Station, it looked like they were coming out the wooden door of a little hut with a thatched roof. The door slammed shut, but it made a hissing sound instead of a loud bang. Jared tried to open it. It was locked. *This is not good.*

"Sarah?"

But Sarah was already several paces ahead of him. As Jared's eyes adjusted to the darkness, he saw they were in the middle of a little village. Cobblestone streets meandered through one- and two-story buildings of old stone walls and tile roofs. The village glowed a quiet blue under the full moon. Although it was night-time, the air still felt warmer than the chilly autumn nights of Odyssey.

Sarah stopped. Jared caught up with her. "Look!"

Sarah whispered. She grabbed Jared's arm and pointed down a side street.

There, out of the darkness, a fiery light was moving toward them! Jared wasn't sure whether to run or stay. Sarah froze. As the light grew closer, it outlined the figure of a man walking toward them. When the man approached, he held up his lantern to see their faces better. The warm glow of the lamp lit up a familiar face with a white mustache.

"Mr. Whittaker!" Jared cried out. "What a relief!"

"Shhhh!" Mr. Whittaker cautioned Jared, a finger to his lips. Mr. Whittaker didn't look relieved to see them at all. In fact, he looked worried. "From the signs I've seen on a couple of buildings, and the style of architecture, we appear to be in some kind of Italian village in the 1600s."

"What's so bad about that?" Sarah asked.

Mr. Whittaker replied, "This isn't my program."

Jared gulped. "What do you mean?"

"I didn't design the adventure we're experiencing right now."

"So . . . ?" Sarah motioned with her hand for Mr. Whittaker to please continue.

"So," Mr. Whittaker said, "to be perfectly honest, I'm not sure what's going to happen to us. I always place safety protocols on each program I design for the Imagination Station. Those protocols allow you to experience everything in your imagination, but within clear safety limits, so that no one gets hurt."

"I think you lost me," said Sarah, with a bewildered look on her face.

"It comes down to this, Sarah," Mr. Whittaker said, "There's no telling who programmed this adventure. It's very possible there are no safety protocols in place at all. That means whatever dangers we face in this adventure could be very real, and could possibly be very dangerous. That's why we've got to get out of the Imagination Station immediately."

"But aren't we outside it already?" asked Sarah.

"No," explained Mr. Whittaker. "All that we're experiencing right now is still *inside* the Imagination Station."

Sarah frowned, a puzzled look in her eye. Jared remembered feeling the same way when he first started asking Mr. Whittaker about how the Imagination Station worked. But Mr. Whittaker didn't stop to explain any further tonight.

He pulled out a small hand-held device from his shirt pocket. It was round with a display screen and several buttons. Jared recognized it as the remote control for the Imagination Station.

"I had trouble with the remote when I first got here. I just hope . . . "

Mr. Whittaker's voice trailed off as he pushed a couple of buttons. A strange frown crossed his face. Jared had never seen this expression on Mr. Whittaker's face before. It was a look that said things were getting out of control.

Mr. Whittaker held up the remote to Jared and Sarah. The bluish-green display lit up one word:

LOCKED

Sarah tapped her chin with her finger. "So this means . . ."

"This means someone has locked us inside the Imagination Station," Mr. Whittaker explained, "and there's no way out."

Jared's eyes bulged.

"But isn't there—" Sarah began. She never finished her sentence. At that very moment, a noise cut through the quiet night air. The sound was unmistakable as it grew louder—the rhythmic cadence of horse hooves on a nearby street. Galloping, galloping, galloping. Closer and closer and closer.

Mr. Whittaker took charge. "Quick, you two hide behind that bush!" Without hesitation, Jared and Sarah followed his orders. And Mr. Whittaker was right behind them. He blew into the lantern. The little flame coughed into a wisp of smoke and disappeared—just in time. Jared peered through the bush. He could see the approaching silhouette of a dark horse against the moonlit walls of the village storefronts. But Jared also spotted something that gave him goose bumps. On the horse's back was a rider, dressed in a dark, hooded robe.

The horse slowed to a trot and stopped, maybe half a block from where Jared and the others were crouching.

The hooded rider turned in their direction. Did he spot them behind the bush?

The rider pulled on the reins; the horse then turned and trotted toward them!

Sarah loved horses and loved to ride them, but the horse heading toward them terrified her. Maybe it was the size of the animal—immense and powerful like a beast from a myth. Or its appearance—dark like the deep of a moonless night. Or maybe it was the rider—mysterious and secretive like a robed ghost.

The Hooded Horseman pulled the reins back, and the black horse obeyed, stopping right in front of the bush.

Sarah held her breath. She glanced at Jared. His eyes were wide. Then, *Beep!*

It was only a little beep, like the sound that one of those digital watches makes when it's at the top of the hour. But to Sarah, it might as well have been a foghorn. It came from the remote control Mr. Whittaker was holding. Fortunately, the horse snorted just when the beep went off, masking the sound almost completely.

Sarah peeked through a little hole in the foliage. The Hooded Horseman dismounted—his motions smooth, steady, and sure. He walked toward a white stucco cottage across the street, its lights asleep in the night.

Sarah glanced over at Mr. Whittaker. He wasn't watching the horse. Instead, he frowned as he stared down at the bluish letters glowing on the remote's display panel. Sarah spotted two words that didn't make sense to her at all:

WHAT
AMATI

What? What's a WHAT? And what's an Amati? Suddenly, a shout shattered Sarah's thoughts. From somewhere inside the cottage, a man's voice called out, *"Che succede? Che succede?"*

The Hooded Horseman ran out of the cottage. In one swift, flowing move, he mounted his horse and quickly slipped the object he was carrying into a saddlebag hanging on the horse's side. Just before the object disappeared into the sack, the moonlight reflected just long enough for them to catch a glimpse of curving wood—the unmistakable shape of a violin.

The Horseman glanced around quickly. He made a clicking sound with his mouth, and the horse galloped away. But just before the horse turned, Sarah noticed something unusual. The horse was branded just above his rear leg. The moonlight caught four digits: 1 1 0 2.

Seconds later, a rather large, black-bearded man stumbled out of the house in a white nightgown. He looked in the direction of the fading hoofbeats and scratched his head.

Sarah was going to ask Mr. Whittaker if they should tell the man what they saw, but Mr. Whittaker quickly held his index finger to his lips.

The round man paused a moment, shook his head, and waddled back inside. His wooden door slammed tight. Sarah heard a bolt slide into place.

Mr. Whittaker started to whisper, and Sarah leaned in to hear better. "As long as we're in this adventure, we've got to keep a low profile. There's no telling who the good guys are and who the bad guys are. I design *my* programs with a moral behind the story, but I don't know if there is *any* moral guiding this program." Sarah thought through this whole mess—the runaway Imagination Station, the mysterious Horseman, the strange village they were in. Her usual spunky attitude had turned into dismay. *This is all just too weird for me to handle.*

"I'd like to go home now," she said firmly.

"That's just it, Sarah," Mr. Whittaker replied. "We *can't* go home until we figure our way out of this adventure."

"But how?" asked Sarah.

"Usually I'm the one who ends the adventure. But

that's when I'm on the *outside,* at the controls. At this point, we have only two ways out: the remote control—which has been locked—and the portal."

Sarah was anxious to learn more. "What's a portal?"

"It's like an escape hatch. I build one into every Imagination Station adventure I program. It's usually a tunnel or a doorway or something like that. If anything malfunctions, you can always head for the portal to escape the program.

"Problem is, I didn't create this program, so I have no idea where the portal is. Or if there even *is* one. And not only is the remote control locked, it's acting strangely. I never designed it to transmit messages like this."

Jared got that wild look in his eye again.

"Oh no," said Sarah. "What are you thinking *now?*"

Jared lifted his index finger to announce his latest theory. "Maybe the two words on the remote control are clues of some kind . . . "

Jared actually made sense this time! Sarah thought.

" . . . sent by a wandering colony of misguided space aliens," Jared continued.

I should have known better.

"I have a hunch you may be right, Jared," Mr. Whittaker said. "Er, about the clue part, anyway. Whoever programmed this adventure could be controlling it right now. He may very well be feeding us clues. I don't know."

"But can this guy be trusted?" Jared asked. "I mean,

can you trust someone who locks you inside the Imagination Station?"

"Good question. Then again, if we go along with the program and figure out the clues, we may be able to find the portal and escape the Imagination Station."

Mr. Whittaker glanced at the display.

WHAT
AMATI

"So what does it *mean?*" Sarah blurted out, an edge of frustration in her voice.

"I don't know," Mr. Whittaker replied, staring at the road for a moment.

He turned to look at both Sarah and Jared, as if sizing up the situation.

"This may be dangerous," he said, "but we've got to track down that Horseman."

"Um, why do we need to do that?" asked Jared, as his voice cracked. He cleared his throat. "I mean, can't we just sit here and figure out the clue? I like word games. And this one may be kind of fun; you never know!" He let out a nervous chuckle.

"I'm afraid that won't work," said Mr. Whittaker. "After all, it was no mistake that we saw the Horseman take the violin. That was by design. It's how the Imagination Station adventure works. The programmer plugs in certain key events. And the way a person responds to those events determines how the adventure goes."

"I understand . . . " Sarah said hesitantly, not at all sure that she really did.

"Someone's trying to tell us something," Mr. Whittaker explained. "For good or for bad, I believe that someone wants us to follow the Horseman. By doing so, we may figure out this clue—and figure out how to escape."

Mr. Whittaker paused. "There's one more thing."

"What's that?" Jared asked.

"The number on the horse. It was significant."

Jared frowned. "You mean the 1102?"

"Yes. 1102 was my agent number."

Jared's eyes lit up. "*Agent number?* You mean you really *were* a—"

"I'm long since retired. But keep that to yourself all the same, would you please?"

Jared—his mouth open with astonishment—nodded a vacant yes. Sarah enjoyed seeing him speechless like that.

Mr. Whittaker glanced around. "For now, I want you two to stay hidden behind this bush. I'm going to look for some kind of transportation—anything. I'll be back as quickly as I can. Don't move!"

Sarah obeyed. Mr. Whittaker headed down the street and ducked around the corner. But just as he disappeared, Sarah heard a noise that made her tingle all over: a groan, deep and long and mournful.

Jared was still in shock over Mr. Whittaker's revelation. But something else grabbed his attention for the moment—that unmistakable groan.

"It sounds like somebody's hurt," Sarah whispered. "It's coming from the woods."

Jared looked behind them into a dark sanctuary of trees.

"Why don't you check it out?" he suggested. "I'll stay here and guard this bush."

"Thank you, O Brave Guardian of the Bush," Sarah chided.

She stepped cautiously toward the woods, and soon her silhouette melted into the night. All was quiet now, except for the crickets. *I really should have gone with her,* Jared thought. *But wait. Mr. Whittaker told us to stay put, so I did the right thing, didn't I?* Jared squinted as he tried to locate her figure in the woods. *Still, I wonder if she's all right. Maybe she—*

Suddenly, something cold and hard clasped his wrist! Jared spun around. A tall, pale-faced man stood behind him, holding a cloth to his head. The man groaned, then removed the cloth to reveal a tiny trickle of blood on his forehead.

That was the last thing Jared remembered. The next thing he knew, he was waking from a semi-comatose state, looking up at Sarah as she waved a scarf over his face.

"You okay?" she asked. Jared was embarrassed. He didn't like seeing blood. Or tall, pale-faced men who groaned in the night.

The voice of a stranger interjected. "I'm sorry, I didn't mean to frighten you."

Jared jumped up and turned around. It was the Massive Head Wound Man! Well, maybe that was a bit of an exaggeration. It was more like a small cut, and it wasn't bleeding anymore. But just thinking about the blood made Jared feel light-headed again.

Jared noticed the man's crisp, dark suit with gray stripes. He remembered seeing one just like it on a mannequin at Greenblatt's Department Store in downtown Odyssey. The man was tall and thin, with a long, angled nose and a full, black mustache under it. Jared guessed he was probably in his fifties.

"How long was I out?" Jared asked.

"A few minutes," Sarah replied.

Jared's head was still spinning. He spotted Mr. Whittaker standing next to a horse and buggy, adjusting the harness. Mr. Whittaker looked over at Jared and called out to him, "So, how's our patient?"

"Confused," Jared answered back.

"And, um, I'm a little confused myself," said the man in the suit. "I know I'm in some kind of virtual adventure machine, but I'm still not quite sure how I got here."

"I want to ask you more about that," Mr. Whittaker said as he checked the reins. "But right now, we've got to catch up to that Horseman we just saw—he's apparently the only way we'll escape."

"I believe I'd like to come with you," said the man. "You may be the only way I can get out of here myself."

"Of course," replied Mr. Whittaker as he tugged on the harness one last time. "C'mon, everyone!" he said as he hopped in the driver's seat. "We're losing time." Mr. Whittaker chuckled to himself. "In fact, I've already lost my watch."

"What happened?" asked Jared as he climbed in the buggy behind the man in the suit.

"I traded it for this horse and buggy. Pretty good deal, don't you think?"

Jared nodded as he looked over the buggy. He was impressed.

"Had to wake up the innkeeper to do it. Maybe he was just trying to get rid of me!" Mr. Whittaker smiled as he grabbed the reins. Sarah climbed up front with

Mr. Whittaker, while Jared and the man in the suit sat in back.

"Giddyap! Yaw, yaw!" shouted Mr. Whittaker. The horse started off with a trot, and the buggy lurched forward.

In the back of the buggy, the man turned to Jared. "I already introduced myself to the others, but I haven't met you," he said with a friendly warmth in his voice. He held out his right hand. "My name is Dr. Maggini."

"*Doctor* Maggini?" Jared said as he grabbed the man's hand. *Wow, what an opportunity!* Jared thought. "Maybe you can help me," he said. "See, I've got this little wart on my left toe that I can't get rid of. I've tried all kinds of medicine and I—"

Sarah interrupted. "He's not *that* kind of doctor, Jared."

"Huh?"

"He's a doctor of music history."

"Oh!" said Jared. He waited a moment. "Still, do you know anything about warts?"

Dr. Maggini shook his head no.

Mr. Whittaker called back over his shoulder. "Dr. Maggini, can you tell us more about how you ended up here?"

"I'd be glad to," said Dr. Maggini. "Actually, I'm from New York. I was invited to Odyssey to present a lecture at Campbell College. And while I was in town, I kept hearing over and over again about John Avery

Whittaker and the Imagination Station. I just had to
visit. So after my lecture, I stopped by Whit's End.
Somebody told me you were upstairs. But when I went
up to find you, you weren't there. Suddenly, out of
nowhere, someone knocked me on the head and
shoved me inside the Imagination Station."

Ah, thought Jared. *That explains the blood.* But he
didn't want to think about it too much.

"I suppose I was knocked unconscious," continued
Dr. Maginni. "I woke up with a splitting headache.
And I'm still trying to figure out what's going on."

"Join the club," said Mr. Whittaker. "All I know for
sure is we're locked inside the Imagination Station until
we can solve this mystery."

Mr. Whittaker paused a moment, then continued.
"Although your being here may give us a clue about
what's going on *outside* the Imagination Station. Did you
see anybody before you were thrown in the machine?"

"No," replied Dr. Maginni. "It happened too fast."

"Hmmm," thought Mr. Whittaker aloud. "So what
was your lecture about?"

"Violins."

Jared piped up. "That's it! I knew it! Don't you see?
This is all about *violence*! Something violent is going to
happen to us!"

"Jared, calm down. He said *violins.*" Mr. Whittaker
let go of the reins just long enough to play an air violin for Jared.

"Oh!" Jared replied. "*Violins!* Okay!" He let out an

embarrassed chuckle. *I still think there's a connection somehow,* he thought.

Mr. Whittaker talked over his shoulder to Dr. Maggini. "As I was telling you earlier, we saw this Horseman take off with a violin. Could this be related to your lecture in some way?"

"It could be," Dr. Maggini said.

Just before the buggy rolled into a deeply forested area, Jared spotted a wooden sign on the other side of the roadway. It was facing backwards.

"What's that sign say, Jared?" Mr. Whittaker asked.

Jared looked back over his left shoulder and squinted. The moonlight lit up the word. "Cremona," said Jared.

Dr. Maggini cried out. "Cremona? This is *Cremona?!*" He laughed. Jared wasn't sure what was so funny.

"Cremona, Italy, is the birthplace of the very finest violins in the world, starting in the 1500s. Ever hear of a Stradivarius violin? They're named after the greatest violin maker of all time, Antonio Stradivari."

Sarah interjected. "Oh yeah. Those violins are worth gobs of money!"

"Yes, I personally know of one that sold for 2.7 million dollars," said Dr. Maggini, one eyebrow raised.

Jared whistled.

Dr. Maggini smiled and continued. "There are legends about people risking their lives just to get their hands on one. But Cremona is also the birthplace of an even more rare violin, one that I think is even more precious. It was crafted by the man who taught Stradivari all that he knew. His name was Nicolo Amati."

Amati?! Jared coughed.

Mr. Whittaker and Sarah said it in unison, almost as if they had rehearsed it. "Amati?!"

"Yes, Amati." Dr. Maggini replied. "Stradivari was his apprentice. Amati was the master violin maker."

"That's the name that showed up on the remote!" Jared exclaimed.

"I'm sorry," said Dr. Maggini with a note of confusion in his voice. "What remote are you talking about?"

Mr. Whittaker retrieved the device from his coat pocket. "This is the remote control to the Imagination Station," he said, handing it back to Dr. Maggini. "Check the display."

Dr. Maggini looked at the remote. His voice was almost hoarse with awe. "Then the violin that was stolen must have been one . . . made by Amati!"

"Exactly!" exclaimed Mr. Whittaker.

"And that must be why I'm here," continued Dr. Maggini, "to help you find this precious Amati violin."

"It's precious for more than one reason," said Mr. Whittaker. "I'm almost certain that violin is our ticket to escape the Imagination Station!" He smiled. "Well, then, the chase is on!"

He gave a loud "YEE-haw!" and the horse charged forward. Jared yelled "WHOAAAAH!" as he fell back clumsily into his seat. The passengers held on to the sides of the buggy as the horse galloped on.

large-framed man with short, curly, gray hair and thick, black eyebrows lay sleeping in the dark. He was tilted back at a comfortable angle in an oversized, tan leather recliner—a recliner traveling at 458 miles an hour, six miles above the black waters of the Atlantic Ocean.

The air whispered past the jet, providing a calming "white noise" to sleep by. The phone imbedded in the right armrest of the chair broke the quiet hush. It rang once, then twice. The man shook his head but never opened his eyes. His hand snatched up the ringing menace and held it against his ear.

"Yeah, what?" he said in a gruff, gravelly voice that rumbled through the darkness.

"I'm sorry to disturb you, Mr. Klaushack," said a thin, youthful voice over the phone, "but you told us to call you if we got any infor—"

"Cut the groveling, Nelson. What's the news?"

"We've tracked him down, sir!" said the voice in the phone.

"Where?"

"A little town called Odyssey," the voice responded.

"And what about the violin? Has he got the violin?"

"We don't know yet, but—"

"Look," said Mr. Klaushack. "You let Wasatchi know that I'm flying there right now to get that violin personally. And when I get there, I'd better not be disappointed." The man's eyes opened. "Do I make myself clear?"

"Yes sir," the voice replied. "Very clear."

The horse galloped down the moonlit roadway as the buggy bounced and jostled its riders. Sarah wasn't sure how long it had been, but it felt like they'd been riding for hours with no horseman in sight. On their right, a little stream joined them in the journey. Sarah looked through the swiftly passing tree branches to see the moonlight sparkle on the water.

Mr. Whittaker gave a silent signal with his reins. The horse slowed down to a trot and stopped beside the stream at a wide clearing on the side of the road. The road itself curved ahead, away from the water. It looked like the last chance to get a drink for a while.

"Our horse needs water and some rest," Mr. Whittaker

said. "Let's take a little break. But keep it short. We need to get going again as soon as possible."

Everybody hopped out of the buggy to stretch their legs.

Finally! Sarah thought, happy to be out of the buggy. *I need a little girls' room—PRONTO!* She noticed a ridge on the other side of the stream—just a little hop over the ridge would provide some nice privacy.

"I've got to, uh, excuse myself," Sarah said quietly to Mr. Whittaker.

"Fine," said Mr. Whittaker. "But be careful," he warned, "and come back quickly."

Sarah crossed the stream, stepping one by one on the rocks that jutted out of the chortling water. She scrambled up the bank, then slipped behind the ridge into a group of thick bushes.

Moments later, as she stepped out of the shrubbery, she heard a noise that caught her attention. *What was that?*

The hill sloped downward to meet a small pond, surrounded by trees. *There it was again.* It sounded like some kind of animal rustling through dead leaves—a big animal.

Then something moved in the shadows by the pond. Sarah wasn't sure if it was real or her imagination. She squinted, trying to see better. *Is it a deer?*

Scared, but curious as always, Sarah inched her way down toward the pond. *I'll just check this out real quick and head right back,* she told herself.

Suddenly, she froze like a statue. Maybe it was fear. Maybe she just didn't want to be discovered. Because now, she could see clearly in the moonlight—the black horse! And just beyond the horse, the Hooded Horseman! His back was toward her as he sat on a rock and sorted through a satchel.

Who is this guy? He could be a kidnapper, for all Sarah knew. And yet, he was also their key to escape the Imagination Station. One wrong move and she could blow their chances of ever getting back home.

Gotta get Mr. Whittaker, she thought as she slowly backed away, all the while keeping her eye on the Horseman. Steadily, she walked backwards up the hill. Slowly . . . carefully . . . one foot at a time. She was only two steps from the top of the ridge when . . . *CRUNCH!* Her foot landed on a little pile of very dry leaves. The Horseman turned around and glared in her direction. Sarah quickly ducked behind the ridge.

She scurried down the slope, waving her arms, silently trying to get Mr. Whittaker's attention.

Minutes later, Mr. Whittaker dashed toward the top of the ridge with Sarah right on his heels. He'd told the others to stay with the horse and buggy.

"Which way?" Mr. Whittaker whispered. Sarah pointed silently to the pond. The Hooded Horseman was still there, but he was standing now, tightening up the saddle on his horse.

"You stay low and stay put," Mr. Whittaker whispered to Sarah. "If I get into trouble, you run back and tell the others, all right?"

"All right," Sarah whispered back as she crouched behind a tree.

Mr. Whittaker took a deep breath and walked toward the pond. He cleared his throat and let out a friendly "Hello there!"

Mr. Whittaker's one brave man, thought Sarah as she watched—and prayed. The Horseman spun around and faced Mr. Whittaker.

"I'm John Avery Whittaker, and I wondered if you could help me with something."

Sarah watched as Mr. Whittaker now steadily made his way to the Horseman. *So far, so good.*

She could barely see Mr. Whittaker as he reached out his hand to greet the Horseman. The Horseman didn't return the handshake, but he did something much more remarkable. He lifted his hand to his hood as if to reveal his identity!

Sarah heard something move behind her. She saw the Horseman glance up in her direction. She turned around and saw Dr. Maggini, peering around a small tree. The Horseman dropped his hand from his hood. Then, with the effortless moves of a dancer, he twirled around and leaped onto the horse—his left foot slid into the stirrup, his right leg swung over. In a flash, the Horseman and his horse were one in flight, disappearing into the shadows of the night.

Mr. Whittaker turned around. Dr. Maggini waved

sheepishly. Sarah knew Dr. Maggini was probably embarrassed, but she was mad at him, too. He had really messed things up.

Mr. Whittaker walked up the hill as Dr. Maggini made his way down to meet him, his face drawn. He shook his head as he called out, "Mr. Whittaker, I apologize—"

Mr. Whittaker interrupted him. "Dr. Maggini, I was very clear when I said I needed you and Jared to stay with the buggy. You could have very well ruined our only chance to get out of the Imagination Station."

"Please," Dr. Maggini said, "please forgive me."

Mr. Whittaker sighed. "I forgive you," he said. "But I'm going to need your help now more than ever."

"I'll do everything I can," said Dr. Maggini, sounding relieved and grateful.

They returned to the buggy and found Jared sprawled on the seat, snoring like an old saw cutting through lumber. Dr. Maggini held Sarah's hand as she jumped into the buggy. Jared snorted and woke up startled. "Huh?!" He sat upright. "I'm on alert, Mr. Whittaker!" he shouted.

"So I see," Mr. Whittaker said with a smile as he grabbed the reins. Dr. Maggini climbed in quickly. Mr. Whittaker let out a loud "Yee-haw! Haw!" And the horse—now fully rested—took off down the path. Faster and faster he galloped into the moonlight shadows.

Sarah felt as if the buggy would come apart as it barreled down the twisting roadway, careening around corners and bouncing off the ground with every bump and dip in the path. She looked in the back of the buggy. Dr. Maggini held on with all his might. Jared's eyes were at half-mast. He looked sick.

They reached a straight part of the road. Sarah saw something on the horizon. The black horse again! The Hooded Horseman dipped down beyond a hill and disappeared.

Mr. Whittaker cracked the reins. "Yaw! Yaw!"

As they bottomed the hill, the road curved to the right. For just a moment, it felt like they were riding on two wheels. Then—*whoa!*—down they went into a steep dip in the road, and back up again just as fast. It felt like Sarah left her stomach on the hill. Meanwhile, Jared was leaning over the side of the buggy like a seasick passenger on a ship.

Just as they rounded another bend, Sarah could see a stone bridge far off in the distance. The Horseman vanished under the archway of the bridge and into the darkness underneath.

Now they headed full-bore toward the bridge—the galloping horse, the rumbling buggy, faster and faster. As they drew closer, Sarah noticed the place under the bridge appeared to be a tunnel.

Her eyes grew wide. "Mr. Whittaker! That could be the portal we've been looking for!"

"Exactly!" yelled Mr. Whittaker. Sarah looked back

at Jared. "Jared, did you hear?" she asked. "This could be it! This could be the portal!"

Jared hung his head over the side and just groaned. Sarah stared ahead. She didn't like tunnels. She hoped it was a short one.

Mr. Whittaker shook the reins, and the horse sped toward the black hole.

ared raised his head just in time to see the bridge ahead. Underneath the archway, it looked like the darkness went on forever. *Is there an end to that tunnel?* Jared wondered.

Suddenly the moonlight faded as the buggy plunged under the archway. The sound of horse hoofs and rolling wheels reverberated in the darkness around them. Jared spotted a brilliant white circle in the distance, getting bigger and bigger as they raced forward.

Moments later, the circle of light exploded over the buggy. They were now outside, surrounded by blinding sunshine bursting out of a vibrant, blue sky. A few long, lazy clouds stretched out and rested on the horizon. Jared looked behind him to see where they had just exited—the tunnel was now a cave cut into a rocky hillside.

"Whoa! Whoa, boy!" Mr. Whittaker tugged on the

reins. The horse slowed to a trot and stopped. The animal panted heavily.

Mr. Whittaker sighed. "Well, that was obviously not the portal."

"And this is obviously not Italy," remarked Dr. Maggini.

Jared took a deep breath. He was feeling better now that the buggy had stopped. As his eyes adjusted to the sudden sunshine, he could see Dr. Maggini was right. This was no Italy. They were on some sort of grassy ridge with a prairie to their left.

Up ahead, the dusty, brown road curved to the right. About a mile off, the road doubled back and descended into a little town below on the right, a town of clapboard-sided buildings, with horses tied to hitching posts and an occasional horse and buggy rumbling through the streets.

But there was no sign of the Horseman anywhere.

"Let's take a little break while we figure out what to do from here," said Mr. Whittaker.

Jared jumped from the buggy first. He turned around and helped Sarah hop down. Dr. Maggini followed. Sarah stretched out her arms in a yawn. Jared leaned against the buggy and sighed. Dr. Maggini walked up to the horse, petting him gently on the nose and reassuring him. "Good boy. You've had quite a run."

Mr. Whittaker remained in the buggy. It looked like he was deep in thought, as if he were trying to sort things out.

"Hmmmm," said Dr. Maggini, "I wonder what town that is."

All eyes looked down below. Jared spotted a cowboy walking down the street—tall and slender, brown cowboy hat and all. "Cool!"

"Maybe this town has something to do with the violin," Sarah mused.

"You think so, Mr. Whittaker?" Jared asked.

"Well, I—"

At that moment, the horse let out a strange, haunting whinny. Dr. Maggini stepped back. The horse kicked. Mr. Whittaker jumped down from his driver's seat and worked quickly to undo the harness from the horse. Jared figured Mr. Whittaker wanted to give the horse some breathing room or something. But it was very difficult to do, since the animal was getting more and more restless.

Finally, the horse broke free. Jared and Sarah tried to keep their distance. All of a sudden, the horse stopped and reared up on its hind legs. Jared's jaw dropped. The gentle horse now seemed like a huge monster towering over him. The horse fell from the sky and slammed to the earth on his front hooves. The impact shook the ground under Jared's feet.

The horse stood motionless for a moment. Jared held his breath. Then the horse's legs buckled under. He collapsed on the ground, raising a large cloud of dust.

Mr. Whittaker rushed over to check on him. Dr. Maggini, Jared, and Sarah gathered beside him as Mr.

Whittaker put his hand on the horse's stomach. "He's still breathing—but he seems to be out cold. Like he's in a deep sleep. This is the strangest thing . . . "

"I don't know much about horses," Dr. Maggini said to Mr. Whittaker. "How about if you stay here while I go into town to find a veterinarian, and maybe another horse for us?"

"Good idea," said Mr. Whittaker. Without another word, Dr. Maggini ran toward the town, taking a shortcut down the hillside.

He wasn't gone long when Jared heard a beep from the buggy. He instantly recognized the sound. While Mr. Whittaker and Sarah watched over the horse, Jared peered into the buggy, looking for . . . *There it is!* The remote control sat on the floor.

"Mr. Whittaker, look at this!" Jared showed the remote to Mr. Whittaker. The display now read:

WHERE
ANDREW

"Andrew . . . Andrew . . . " Mr. Whittaker rubbed his chin. "If we can just figure out who and where Andrew is, we may be able to find that violin," he said.

"I'd like to know who's sending us these clues, anyway?" wondered Sarah aloud.

"Good question."

Jared half-listened to Mr. Whittaker and Sarah. He was working out his own theories. *Andrew . . . Andrew . . .*

Sarah piped up. "Maybe it's the owner of the violin, and he wants us to find it for him," she said. "Or it could be a bad guy who's trying to trap us."

"Could be," said Mr. Whittaker.

Andrew . . . Andrew . . . Jared mulled the name over in his mind. "Maybe there's an Andrew in that town down there!" he said. "Maybe the Horseman hid the violin in the town! Maybe this town is an ancient UFO landing site!"

Jared didn't have a chance to explain his spectacular theory—and it was a good one, too—because Sarah suddenly cried, "Look! He's awake!"

Before Jared could blink, the horse stood up. Mr. Whittaker motioned for Jared and Sarah to back away. The horse had a wild look in his eye. Then, in a flash, he bolted for the prairie.

Mr. Whittaker spoke first. "Well, there's no sense in waiting here now," he said as he watched the horse run farther and farther away, disappearing into the gentle hills of the prairie. "Let's head to town. Like Dr. Maggini said, we may be able to find another horse, or possibly some clues to the violin. We'll probably run into Dr. Maggini on the way, so we need to keep our eyes open for him. Jared, you hold on to that remote."

"Yes sir," said Jared, putting on his most responsible "You can count on me!" voice. He tucked the remote into his shirt pocket.

They hiked through the downward slope of tall, yellow grass, the same shortcut Dr. Maggini had taken.

The warm wind reached out of the wide-open sky and tousled Jared's hair. It always amazed Jared how *real* everything felt in the Imagination Station.

Before long, the three entered the town itself. Maybe twenty or thirty people strolled the dirt street, some riding horses, some walking, others driving carriages or buggies. Jared noticed most of the men wore cowboy hats. The ladies wore humongous dresses that, from the waist down, looked like really fancy parachutes.

A little kid chased an oinking pig down one of the wooden sidewalks that lined the street. People stepped aside as the kid came bursting through, shouting at the pig, "Come back here, you!" A couple of the cowboys laughed.

Now and then someone walked into or out of the wood-framed shops on either side. There was a sign for a "Gentlemen's Clothier" on the right, next to a "General Store." On the left was a "United States Postal Office" and "Fred the Haberdasher." Jared was trying to figure out what a haberdasher did. *Sounds like somebody who makes habers really, really fast.* But before he could figure out what a haber was, Mr. Whittaker gasped.

"What is it?" Sarah asked.

"I recognize this street from some old photos I've seen," Mr. Whittaker said as he looked around. "This isn't just any old Western town," he said. "This is *Odyssey!*"

8

Sure enough, Sarah thought. As they walked along the street, a large ornate clock tower seemed to emerge above the other buildings. Sarah pointed out Odyssey's famous landmark. "City Hall!"

"Cool!" Jared said. "And look, there's the Odyssey Hotel!" Across the street from City Hall sat the town's first lodging place, one that still stood in modern-day Odyssey on the corner of McAlister and Main.

Sarah thought it was fascinating to walk down Main Street just as it was more than one hundred and fifty years ago. She wanted to explore every shop and talk to every person she met.

"Can we look around?" Sarah asked.

"I'm just as curious as you are," Mr. Whittaker said, "but we've all got to keep an eye out for Dr. Maggini."

"Oh. Right." Sarah said. "And the Horseman," she added.

"And the violin," said Jared.

Sarah sighed. "But what does Andrew *mean?*"

"Hmmm," said Mr. Whittaker. Then a smile crossed his face. "Of course!"

"What is it?" Sarah asked.

"Now that we know this is Odyssey, I think I've just figured out what our clue means," he said. "Back in the mid 1800s—the very same time period we're in now—a pastor named Reverend Andrew lived on the site of what's now Whit's End. He was also part of the Underground Railroad."

Jared made the connection. "Was he the one who helped slaves escape through the secret tunnel under Whit's End?" Jared asked.

"That's right," Mr. Whittaker said. "And Reverend Andrew's tunnel is the only part of the rectory that's survived to present-day Whit's End."

Sarah wrapped it up. "So the violin is . . . ?"

"In the tunnel!" Jared exclaimed.

"That's what I'm thinking," said Mr. Whittaker.

Oh boy, Sarah thought. *Another tunnel?*

"You know," Mr. Whittaker continued, "only a few people know about that tunnel. And one of them is Don."

"Who's Don?" Jared asked as Mr. Whittaker led them down a quiet side street.

"Don Cortado. He's the friend I told you about," said Mr. Whittaker. "The one who disappeared."

"Whoa. Do you think he's connected somehow?"

"I don't know. But we need to get to Reverend Andrew and find that violin. I have a hunch someone may be trailing us."

Sarah looked over her shoulder. A dark brown horse, tied up to one of the posts, stared back at them. The wind caught some tumbleweed and rolled it across the dusty street. It looked like the opening scene from one of those old Western movies. But where was the guy in the black hat?

Mr. Whittaker pointed ahead of them. "If I remember my history right, there's a livery stable up around Peagram Street. Let's go!"

"Um," started Jared nervously, "I think my liver is perfectly normal. You can ask my doctor. He said he's never seen a healthier—"

"Jared!" Sarah groaned. "A livery stable is where they keep *horses*."

"Oh. Then why don't they call it something that makes sense—like a used horse lot?"

"*You* don't make sense," said Sarah.

"All right, you two," scolded Mr. Whittaker. "Sarah, have you ridden a horse before?"

"Yes, sir," said Sarah. "I ride one at my cousin's farm all the time."

Mr. Whittaker turned to Jared. "How about you?"

"Um, well, actually, there was . . . "

"Jared? You can ride with me out to Reverend Andrew's house, all right?"

"Great."

"Maybe Dr. Maggini already stopped here to get us a horse," Sarah guessed.

"Good thinking," said Mr. Whittaker. "I'll ask. In the meantime, you two stay here and keep a lookout for him."

Sarah leaned back on a hitching post. It was good just to rest for a moment. She watched as Jared scanned the street with an eye of suspicion.

"What's with you?" Sarah asked.

"Mr. Whittaker said there might be someone following us. So, I'm keeping a lookout."

"Whatever," said Sarah. She leaned back again and closed her eyes.

"Hey," Jared whispered. "That horse over there keeps staring at me. You think it means something?"

"Yes," said Sarah, still resting her eyes, "it means you're loony."

"Ha!" scoffed Jared. "You obviously don't watch many movies."

Sarah tried to ignore Jared, but he didn't pick up the hint. "I saw a movie once about this pack of rabid Chihuahuas who would sneak out from the alley under the cover of night and— AAAAAAAAAAAAAAAAH!"

Sarah's eyes popped open.

Jared yelled, "It's got my leg!"

She looked down at a ball of tumbleweed that had brushed up beside him.

"Oh," Jared chuckled nervously as he kicked away the tumbleweed. "Um . . . just testing out my scream. You know, in case we get into trouble."

"Oh. Good idea," said Sarah with a note of sarcasm.

"Yep, you never know when I could be called upon to scream. A guy's gotta be ready at all times."

"Jared?"

"Yeah?"

"You are hopeless."

A little electronic alarm beeped. It felt out of place in this old western town. Sarah recognized the sound immediately. "Jared! The remote control!"

"I know, I know!" said Jared as he fumbled for the device in his shirt pocket. They looked at the blue display. It spelled out something strange.

5317

"What's 5317?" Sarah asked.

"I don't know," said Jared.

Sarah heard the sound of horse hooves approaching. She looked up from the display.

"Maybe it's some kind of code," said Jared, his eyes glued to the numbers. But Sarah didn't hear him. Her mouth went dry. She tugged at Jared's shirt sleeve.

"What?" Jared snapped.

But Sarah didn't answer.

Jared looked up.

Heading toward them was a dark horse. There was no mistaking the horse. And there was no mistaking the rider.

"Stay right where you are!"

It was the first time Sarah had heard him speak. The

commanding voice of the Hooded Horseman had a tinge of Hispanic accent. Sarah made a mental note. *The police would want to know something like that. If we ever get to the police, that is.*

The black horse now stood before them. The Hooded Horseman towered over them, his face cloaked.

Apparently, Jared's heroic screamer was out of commission. It was her turn. She yelled as loudly as she could, "MR. WHITTAKER!"

The Horseman dismounted. Jared just stood there like an ice sculpture. Sarah caught a glimpse of the Horseman's face—tan-skinned, with a thin mustache.

He spoke quietly, yet with a firm resolve. "It won't do any good to yell. Mr. Whittaker was kidnapped."

"Mr. Whittaker?" Jared said. The news seemed to wake Jared up out of his frozen state. He found his voice. "What have you done with him?" he challenged.

"Nothing," the Horseman said.

"I don't believe you! Tell us where he is!" Jared shot back. Sarah was surprised. This was *Jared?* She wouldn't admit this out loud, of course, but she was proud of his newfound courage. It took a lot to say anything to a tall, overpowering figure cloaked in a dark hood.

The Horseman answered. "Just remember the verse."

Jared frowned. "What verse?"

"Hold it right there!" a familiar voice bellowed. It was Dr. Maggini!

"I'm not going to allow you to hurt these kids!" He walked up from behind Sarah and Jared and now stood between the Hooded Horseman and them. The Hooded Horseman stood unruffled, unmoved, as if in defiance. Dr. Maggini reassured the kids. "It's all right. I'll make sure this thief doesn't harm either one of you."

The Horseman looked straight at Dr. Maggini and spoke under his breath. "You traitor."

Wait. These two know each other? Sarah wondered.

"*I'm* being called a traitor—by a thief?" Dr. Maggini countered. His voice was angry.

"Make that a traitor and a criminal," said the Horseman.

"All right, that's enough!" said Dr. Maggini. "You know very well that violin belongs in a museum. So do the right thing and turn it over. Now."

"You're full of 5317!" the Horseman replied.

Sarah and Jared looked at each other. That was the mysterious number on the remote control! How did the Horseman know that?

"5317?" Dr. Maggini said suspiciously. "What are you talking about?" He stepped toward the Horseman.

Sarah gulped. The man in the hood stood silent. She prayed quietly under her breath.

Suddenly, Dr. Maggini lunged toward him. Sarah gasped. And the Horseman vanished! Just like that, he was *gone!* Dr. Maggini looked around, but there wasn't a trace of him anywhere. His horse was all that was left.

"Whoa!" exclaimed Sarah.

"Remember we're in the Imagination Station," said Jared. "Anything can happen. That's why we've got to get out of here!"

"Hold on!" said Sarah. She had just remembered something about the first time they saw the Hooded Horseman. She looked at the Horseman's horse, her eyes on the saddlebag.

Jared's eyes tracked with hers. "The violin!"

Dr. Maggini's face brightened. "The violin?!"

Sarah ran to the saddlebag. She loosened the buckle, yanked back the strap, and reached in to grab . . . nothing. It was gone. She groaned in frustration.

Dr. Maggini sighed a deep sigh.

"Rats!" said Jared.

Dr. Maggini frowned as if an idea had occurred to him. "Did any more clues show up on the remote control?"

"Oh, yeah," Jared said. "There was WHERE–ANDREW and that weird number, 5317. We don't know what the number means, but we figured out that ANDREW means Reverend Andrew. We're guessing the violin is in the secret tunnel Reverend Andrew built under the rectory around this time period."

Dr. Maggini stroked his chin as if trying to piece it all together.

Jared frowned. "So you know this Horseman?"

Dr. Maggini nodded. "There's a lot I can't tell you just yet, Jared. You'll have to trust me."

Sarah smiled. She knew Jared hated when adults said stuff like that. Jared wanted to know *everything*, especially when it came to secrets and mysteries and elaborate government conspiracies.

Apparently, Dr. Maggini needed to know some things himself. "Where did you last see Mr. Whittaker?"

"He went in there," Jared said, pointing to the livery stable behind them.

"The Horseman may be in there," Dr. Maggini murmured. "This could be a trap of some sort." He paused, then said with resolve, "I'm going inside. You both stay right here. If you see the Horseman again, yell for me, all right?"

Sarah nodded.

"Yes sir," said Jared. With a creak of the front door, Dr. Maggini disappeared into the livery stable.

Sarah felt a bit uneasy about all this. First Mr. Whittaker had disappeared. Then the Horseman. *Who's next? Dr. Maggini? One of us?*

She looked around nervously. Jared handed her the remote control. "See if *you* can make anything of it."

Sarah stared at the numbers—5317—but they still didn't make sense. Just then, Jared inhaled sharply. She looked up—was the Horseman back? No. Jared was staring wide-eyed at the remote in her hand, reading the upside-down display.

"You see it?!" Jared said excitedly.

"No," replied Sarah.

"Here, turn it upside down!" Jared said. He turned the remote around in Sarah's hand.

And there it was!

LIES

5317 spelled LIES! *Now just plug in the clue, like a math equation,* thought Sarah. "So," she blurted, "the Horseman said Dr. Maggini was full of . . . lies!"

Jared leaned against a post and thought through the possibilities out loud. "So was the Horseman telling the truth? Or was *he* lying?" His eyes began to sparkle.

Here we go, thought Sarah.

"Hmmm . . . maybe the Horseman was a virtual hologram!" said Jared. "Then again, maybe *Dr. Maggini* was a virtual hologram! Maybe *you* are, Sarah! Yikes, maybe *I'm* a hologram! Oh *no!*"

"Uh, think we should check inside?" Sarah asked, nodding toward the livery stable. "Dr. Maggini's been gone a while."

"Maybe Dr. Maggini's been kidnapped, too!" Jared said.

"Let's find out," Sarah said, as she opened the door to the stable.

The jet was a whispering thunder over the twinkling lights of sleeping towns below.

Inside, the recessed lights in the cabin lit up a well-furnished miniature kitchen with a microwave, small refrigerator, and stainless steel sink. On the other side of the cabin, a bank of tiny red, blue, and yellow lights surrounded a satellite communications system, complete with a large-display computer monitor and an impressive array of switches, knobs, and buttons.

The tan recliner was upright now, with Mr. Klaushack fully awake—a club soda in his cup holder on the left armrest, the phone in his right hand.

"You tell Wasatchi I've got the money, and I'll fly him anywhere. But I must have the violin."

"The problem is, Mr. Wasatchi says things are getting too hot to carry it around," replied the voice on the other end of the phone line. "Some guy named Whittaker was on to him. There may be more."

Mr. Klaushack leaned forward. "Did you say *Whittaker?*"

"Yes, sir. John Whittaker, I believe."

"Number 1102." Klaushack chuckled. "Now this makes things much more interesting."

"Sir?"

"Oh, nothing. Just an old account I need to settle." Klaushack took a sip of his drink. "All right. Here's the deal. I want the list and I want Whittaker. And tell Wasatchi I'm cutting the payment by one-third."

"But I don't think he'll—"

"That's not negotiable."

Klaushack slammed the phone into the armrest.

In the front room of the livery stable, kerosene lanterns hung from the ceiling. A long, crude wooden counter stood before Jared and Sarah. *It definitely* smells *like a stable,* Jared thought. *Yuck.*

CLANG—CLANG! Jared could hear a hammer banging on something metal. Horseshoes, maybe? Jared tried to peek through the doorway behind the counter. No sign of Dr. Maggini. Or Mr. Whittaker.

A tall man in his late twenties, with a freckled face and reddish hair, emerged from the doorway. "Can't believe how busy things are today!" he remarked as he pulled off thick leather gloves to reveal two huge hands. He shot a hand out to Jared. "I'm Red Johnston," he said, smiling. Jared shook his hand. "What can I do for you kids?"

"We're looking for two people," said Jared. "One's kind of a big guy with white hair, a white mustache, and glasses."

"Oh, yeah!" said Red. "He came in here to check on a horse. I told him to look out back in the stables to see what he wanted." He shook his head, puzzled. "I haven't seen him since. Like he up and disappeared or somethin'."

Jared made a mental note for his theory about Mr. Whittaker being a hologram. "We're also looking for a tall guy dressed in a suit," Jared added, playing the part of a virtual detective.

"You're Jared and Sarah, right?"

Jared and Sarah nodded.

But how does Red know this? Jared wondered suspiciously. *Hmmm. Red doesn't look like a space alien. But then again, you can never be certain . . .*

"Dr. Maggini told me you'd be checking in on him," Red continued.

"Oh," said Jared. *Scratch the alien theory . . .*

"He wanted to borrow one of my horses, so he gave me this real fancy telegraph machine." Red held up a cell phone. "And he told me to give you a message."

"What is it?" Sarah asked.

"He said he was sorry to leave so quickly, but he had an emergency."

"Emergency?" asked Jared.

"He said not to worry, though. He'll be right back. Just wait for him out front there."

Jared wasn't sure if he wanted to wait. "Can we, like, rent a horse?" he asked.

Sarah chimed in. "We have to get to Reverend Andrew's house right away."

"What is goin' on at the Reverend's? That's what I'd like to know," said Red.

"What do you mean?" asked Sarah.

"Both those guys you mentioned said they were headin' out to his place. And now you kids are, too."

Jared looked at Sarah. She looked back. *This is getting weirder all the time,* Jared thought.

"We don't know what's going on," he said, "but we've got to get there fast."

"Well, I'm awful sorry, but I don't rent horses to kids," Red said.

Jared sighed. Sarah piped up. "Could we please have a lump of sugar before we go?"

Jared frowned. *A lump of sugar?* He'd heard that horses like lumps of sugar, but what good would that do? Red thought for a moment, then reached under the counter and pulled out a white cube.

"Here you go. Now you kids shoo 'cause I've got a lotta work to do, hear?"

"Yes, sir," said Sarah and Jared. "And thank you!" added Sarah, tugging on Jared's arm.

She led Jared outside.

"We'll just borrow *this* horse, then," Sarah said, gesturing to the huge dark companion of the Hooded Horseman. She offered the lump of sugar to the horse, and he took to her kindly, nuzzling his nose against her cheek.

Even though Sarah was a girl, Jared was pretty impressed with her resourcefulness. Of course, he didn't want to actually *compliment* her. She seemed to get a big head about stuff like that.

"C'mon," Sarah called, pointing to the stirrup.

"Um, is this really all right to 'borrow' a horse?" asked Jared.

"Good point!"

Sarah pulled a pen out of her pocket and scrounged around the saddlebag for a scrap of paper. After she scribbled something down, she stuck it on a nail protruding from the hitching post:

Dear Mr. Horseman,
Sorry, but we had to borrow your horse. I hope you don't mind, but it's a life and death kind of thing. He's at Rev. Andrew's house.

Thank you very much!
Sarah

"Okay, *now* are you ready?" asked Sarah.

Oh boy, Jared thought. *And I thought I had the perfect stalling tactic.* He had always pretended to be Mr.

Cowboy Hero around horses. But the truth was, he had been bucked by a wild hobbyhorse when he was five. He'd been scared to death of horses ever since.

"We can't wait all day out here," Sarah prodded. "You *do* know how to ride, don't you?"

"Sure! I mean, all you gotta do is put your foot in this thingy down here and hold onto the thingy up here and kinda swing over your leg and sit on the sitter thingy. But hey, aren't girls supposed to go first?" Jared offered the most gentleman-like smile he could muster.

"Only if the boy doesn't know how to ride," Sarah said smugly.

Ouch. How did she know that?

"Oh, never mind," she said. "Just jump on behind me. Let's go!"

Jared noted carefully how Sarah got on the horse, and he tried to mimic her every movement. He started out well, until he swung up his leg and kicked the horse. The horse whinnied and reared up a bit.

"Jared!" Sarah chided.

"I'm on, I'm on," Jared said as he finally settled behind Sarah on the saddle. They started down the dusty street. Jared was familiar enough with Odyssey's history to spot certain buildings and landmarks, and show Sarah which way to go. Without his knowledge, they would have ridden beautifully—in circles. Then again, without Sarah's horseback-riding skills, they would have walked.

Jared looked left and right as they trotted along. He knew Odyssey Community Church was built in the

1800s. If he located the church, he could triangulate its coordinates with the mental global positioning map that he kept in his head specifically for situations just like this (simulated time-traveling catastrophes). In nonspy language, that meant he knew where Whit's End—and Reverend Andrew's house—would be.

"There it is!" said Jared. The little white chapel looked a lot smaller, though. Jared thought back. A few months ago, he had checked out the black-and-white pictures that hung in the church office while he waited for his mom to finish choir practice. He recalled the picture of the Sunday school annex that was built in 1921—and the chapel that was remodeled and expanded in 1947.

He knew exactly where they were now. "Go right! Up Maple Street!" he shouted. They trotted past the Memorial Hospital—or at least where it would have been if they were back home in their own time. Now around the corner from the cemetery—there was McAlister Park. It was only a matter of time . . .

And there it was. Next to a church sat a yellow, two-story wood-frame house with white trim and a wide porch wrapped around it. It looked just like the painting that hung in the Odyssey Public Library.

"Reverend Andrew's house!" Jared cried. He was looking at the future site of Whit's End!

Out front, a gray horse was tied to the white picket fence that surrounded the property. After Sarah gracefully dismounted the horse they were riding (and Jared jumped and tripped, stumbled and toppled off), Sarah tied it up next to the other horse.

"It feels kinda weird around here," Sarah said.

Jared was still spread-eagle on the ground, nursing many wounds, including his pride. He rolled over. The front door of Reverend Andrew's house was wide open. It *did* seem strangely quiet around the place.

But something stranger was happening. It started as a little breeze kicking up some fallen leaves around the house. Then, without any warning—and much quicker than any storm Jared had ever seen—the breeze turned into a fierce and vicious wind. It whipped out of the sky and pummeled the trees. Like a mean-tempered wrestler, it bent the trees without mercy and ripped off their leaves bit by bit. Branches broke off and flew through the air. Columns of dust swirled around in a twisting dance. And the sky changed colors, from blue to green to red to yellow. Jared got on his feet. The color changes grew more rapid. *This doesn't look good.*

The horses pawed the ground nervously.

"What's going on?" Sarah shouted above the wind.

"I don't know!" Jared shouted back just as a bright-green lightning streak split open the sky. Overhead was an ocean of swirling, violent whirlpools of changing, spinning colors.

CRACKKK! Their dark horse broke off a wooden fence slat and galloped off in fear, the rope and the white fence slat dangling at his side. The gray horse also tugged at his rope. Sarah—her hair flying in her face—struggled to untie the horse and set him free.

Now the whole sky pulsated red. Red, black. Red, black. A computerized voice came out of the sky with a warning: "Malfunction. Malfunction." Jared knew that voice well. He shouted, "It's the Imagination Station computer! Something's wrong!"

"Oh, you think so?" Sarah shot back sarcastically.

Jared ignored her attitude. "If the computer goes down, we may *never* get out of here!"

"So what do we do?"

Jared looked at the open front door. He could see nothing beyond it except darkness. A thought struck him. "C'mon!" he said as he grabbed Sarah's hand. There was no time to explain, and it was too windy to hear. He ran with Sarah up the front porch steps, just as the gray horse broke free and vanished down the street in a full gallop.

"Warning. Hardware integrity compromised." The computer voice continued, "Warning. System error."

"Sounds like it's going to crash!" Jared shouted as they reached the front door. He wasn't sure if Sarah heard him. The whole house was creaking and moaning. Sarah hesitated.

"Sarah!" Jared shouted, "This could be it! This could be the portal we've been looking for!"

He didn't wait for her answer. He pulled her inside and slammed the door shut.

Nothing happened. And it was dark. *Whoops. At least I* thought *it was* the portal.

"Okay, Mr. Hero, where is the portal?" Sarah asked.

"Um, I know it's here somewhere," Jared replied. "I think." Jared couldn't see anything. But he could hear the strange storm raging around them outside as branches and unknown objects hit the sides of the house with an occasional BANG! or THUD!

The house uttered a great groan, like the sound an old wooden ship makes in a rough ocean. Suddenly, he felt the whole building lurch! The jolt was so strong, Sarah fell down with a yelp. Jared, still holding her hand, picked her back up. Somewhere upstairs, a window crashed. Then another. And then came a roar like a jet engine winding up. Jared remembered what his Aunt Ruth had told him about that sound. She had grown up on a Kansas farm and knew it well.

"Tornado!" Jared screamed. "Hold on tight!"

The sound rose in pitch and volume—higher and more intense. There was a dull explosion below the house—in the basement maybe?—that was more felt than heard, as if a huge tree trunk had cracked in two. Then it felt like the whole house was spinning around them. Jared and Sarah both fell down, and Sarah's hand slipped from Jared's as they separated in the darkness. Jared hit his elbow hard on something—he didn't know what. The floor tilted violently, and he slid across it. With a bone-bruising THUD, he slammed against a wall. In the darkness, he heard dishes crash to the floor, pictures fall off the wall, furniture snapping like twigs. And the roar! The terrible roar was like a constant thunder that never went away.

He couldn't hear Sarah at all. *Is she all right? Are we gonna make it out of here?*

And then, gradually, the whirring sound dropped in pitch, and the swirling sensation slowed down, like a merry-go-round running out of steam.

The house jolted again as if it had "landed." Jared heard what sounded like a rifle shot.

"Sarah?" he called.

He heard her groan in the darkness.

"Sarah, are you okay?"

A familiar but woozy voice replied, "I think so."

"Sarah, I think we found the escape portal."

"Oh, joy."

"You know what?" said Jared, "I recognize that shot we just heard." He didn't wait for a response. "It's the door lock on the Imagination Station!"

"You . . . you think so?" Sarah was beginning to get her voice back.

"Yeah. But for some reason, the door isn't opening."

The computer voice was now directly overhead. "Warning. Hard drive crash imminent. Exit immediately! Exit immediately!"

"So how are we supposed to 'exit immediately'?" Jared asked. It was totally dark. Even if he could see the door, it wasn't budging.

"Dear God," Jared said, "help us!"

"*Now* you think of praying," scolded Sarah.

And then came more noises that Jared had never heard before in the Imagination Station. Crackling sounds—like electricity—and a deep spiraling-down sound, as if someone had cut the power to a massive machine. And finally, the sound of someone bashing on metal with a heavy tool—CLANG! CLANG!—just like the horseshoes being forged in the livery stable. The metallic thud echoed throughout the dark cavern of the machine.

But this was no horseshoe being forged in a shop. Someone was destroying the Imagination Station!

CLANG! BONG! BASH!

Sarah was getting a headache from the constant noise outside the Imagination Station. And then, all of a sudden, it stopped.

A tiny light appeared ahead in the darkness—a tiny, dim, yellow light. "Look!" said Jared. "It's the dashboard of the Imagination Station!"

Even though the "AUX POWER" light was small, Sarah's eyes were so used to the dark by now that she could see the entire dashboard glowing from the one miniature bulb.

"So if the dashboard is there," Sarah surmised, "that must mean the door is right . . . *here!*"

"Stay back," warned Jared. He aimed his shoulder into the dark and slam-tackled the door like a linebacker.

"Ow," he said quietly.

Sarah watched as a sliver of vertical light split the darkness. Jared grunted, and he slid back the heavy door with all his might.

"After you, Sarah!" he said dramatically.

At last, Sarah stepped outside the Imagination Station! And it wasn't into another adventure, either. It was right back in the ol' Bible Room! *Air! Fresh—what?*

After being in the stuffy machine so long, Sarah wanted so much just to take a deep breath. But all she could do was cough. Jared was coughing, too. The air was filled with smoke and dust and smells—smells of burning wires and melting plastic. Sarah cupped her hand over her nose and mouth as she tried to breathe. They stumbled through the cloud. Glass crunched under their feet.

On their way to the door, Sarah saw the control console to the Imagination Station lying on the floor, or what was left of it. Buttons and knobs were smashed. Wires stuck up in the air like burnt twigs after a forest fire. The Imagination Station itself looked like it had been in a wreck with a semi-truck. Through the smoke, Sarah spotted a crowbar lying in the corner of the Bible Room.

If someone did this to the Imagination Station, what will they do to us? she thought as she looked back at the machine. Mr. Whittaker's door was open . . . but there was no one inside. She coughed. "Where's Mr. Whittaker?" The smoke was really getting to her. "You think he's okay?"

"I wish I knew," Jared said.

"Well," said Sarah with another cough, "thank you, God, for getting us back safely!"

"Amen," said Jared listlessly as they started into the dark hallway.

"So what is going on here?" Sarah wondered aloud.

"I dunno. But it looks like we just barely made it out of the Imagination Station alive."

"Wow," said Sarah.

"C'mon," Jared called. "Let's go find Mr. Whittaker!"

They stepped deeper into the hallway. It was eerily quiet now. Most of the lights were off as they made their way through the dark passageway to the stairs.

A muffled "beep" came from Jared's jacket pocket. He stopped and pulled out the remote control. Sarah looked with Jared at the display:

ISAM 167

Now the bright blue letters and numbers faded to black as if the batteries were dying. Or maybe the Imagination Station itself was dying.

"So what's *that* supposed to mean?" Sarah asked.

"These clues are getting—" Jared put his hand up, interrupting her. They stopped on the stairs. Sarah listened. Listened . . . to the hum of the freezer in the kitchen downstairs . . . to the quiet buzz of the EXIT sign as it lit the hallway in a green glow. And somewhere upstairs, she heard the quiet crunch of glass.

Jared nodded his head. He heard it too. Someone was in the very room they had just left!

Jared cleared his throat and spoke a bit too loudly. "Okay, let's check out that tunnel!" Sarah instantly understood. Whoever it was, Jared was trying to throw them off. He stepped quietly and quickly down the stairs to the main level, with Sarah right behind him. At the bottom, he pointed in the direction of the Kids' Radio Studio. Quickly, they both ducked inside. Jared silently shut the soundproof door.

He slowly slid up the wall like a police detective— well, at least the ones on TV—and stealthily peeked out the little square window in the door. He quickly ducked. "I just saw a shadow pass by," he whispered to Sarah.

He moved up the wall police-detective style again. Then he turned to Sarah with another hushed report. "The door to the basement is open now. It wasn't before."

"Are you sure no one can hear us in here?" Sarah asked softly.

"Yeah, this studio is soundproof," Jared whispered back. "Still, let's keep it quiet just in case."

"So who was it?"

"I have no idea. I couldn't see him."

Something occured to Sarah. "Jared, don't you think it's kinda weird that our parents aren't here, looking for us? I mean, we've been gone for—what?—twenty-four hours or something like that?"

"Nah. It just *feels* that long. Remember? That's what the Imagination Station does. It expands virtual time, so a day or two might be just five or ten minutes of real time. That's what's so cool about it. Or *used* to be cool."

"So we're back on real time now," Sarah said.

"Right. Which means we've gotta hurry up and find that violin before anybody else does."

"Who cares about the violin now?" countered Sarah. "We've got to find Mr. Whittaker."

"Right. And what leads do we have?"

Jared didn't wait for an answer. "I couldn't have said it better myself," he said. "The only connection we have is the violin. If we find it, we may be able to find Mr. Whittaker *and* Dr. Maggini. And hey, it's all we have to go on so far, besides that ISAM 167 thing."

"All right, all right," Sarah replied. "So let's put the clues together."

Jared paced the room.

Sarah started it off. "Okay, WHAT–AMATI. The WHAT is the Amati violin." She found a notebook in the studio and grabbed a pen. At the top of the pad, she tried to work out the last clue . . .

ISAM 167
I SAM

. . . while Jared went through the other clues. "So, the WHERE–ANDREW clue is the secret tunnel," he said as he continued to pace.

"Then we've got LIES," Jared added. Sarah wrote ISAM upside down.

MASI

Then she wrote it backward:

MASI

"But we're not sure yet *who's* lying," Jared went on. "The Hooded Horseman or Dr. Maggini."

"Right," Sarah agreed as she continued playing with the word.

"And now we have ISAM 167," Jared said.

"I can't figure this one out at all," Sarah said as she put down her pen. "So I guess you're right. The only clear lead we have here is the violin in the tunnel."

"Which means," said Jared with difficulty, "we need to . . ."

"Go down to the basement," Sarah completed his sentence. "Right."

"Yeah," replied Jared, his expression displaying all the gusto of a slug.

Sarah grabbed a flashlight from the studio desk.

Ever so cautiously, they descended the stairway to the basement. Sarah was listening at every step.

ared tiptoed through the basement, right behind Sarah and her flashlight. The light beam scanned the large room as they meandered through a maze of strange shapes draped in dust covers. Underneath the sheets were Mr. Whittaker's many inventions and prototypes he had worked on over the years. Jared remembered this from his last visit to the basement with Nick.

Sarah pointed the beam of light toward a black hole in the wall ahead. A tall antique dresser was off to the left, askew, as if it had been pushed it aside. Someone had found the secret tunnel!

Sarah stopped.

"What?" Jared asked.

She didn't have to say anything. Jared saw what stopped her. On the floor was a red puddle.

"It's fake blood," Sarah whispered. "I think."

It's fake. It's fake. Jared tried to tell himself over and over, but he was already feeling woozy. Sarah noticed.

"Jared! Get a hold of yourself!"

Jared barely heard her. The room was tossing around like a great ship pitching on the ocean.

"Oh, boy," said Sarah. "Come on."

Sarah led Jared to an overstuffed armchair a few feet away. He plopped into it, and dust rose like a mushroom cloud. He coughed.

"Just what I thought," Sarah said. Jared didn't care what she thought. He was fading to black . . . checking out . . . hitchhiking to oblivion . . .

"Jared!" Sarah implored, "Don't faint on me *now*! C'mon! It's only food coloring! Look!" She held up a bottle. "This was over in the corner."

Although Jared's eyes were crossed, he could still see the words as Sarah held up the flashlight and read the label aloud. "See? 'Dr. Queezy's 100% Genuine Artificial Blood. For Special Effects Only. Not to be donated.'"

"Artificial?" Jared said weakly. Then he remembered something. "Hey, Sarah," he said hoarsely.

"Yeah?"

"Remember the first time we saw Dr. Maggini?"

"Uh huh."

"Remember he had blood on his . . . his . . . "

Jared's head swirled. In his semi-unconscious state, he heard Mr. Whittaker's voice from Sunday school . . .

"That's right. Appearances can be deceiving. Sarah, what's the Bible verse we're studying this week?"

Sarah's voice echoed in Jared's brain. "Man looks at the outward appearance, but the Lord looks at the heart. First Samuel 16:7 . . . First Samuel 16: 7 . . . First Sam . . ."

SMACK!

Ouch! Jared felt someone slap him in the face!

"Jared, quit fainting on me!"

It was Sarah. But her voice didn't do that echo thing anymore. Had he been dreaming? He opened his eyes. Sarah stood over him with a look of disdain. Apparently, he had fainted.

"Some nurse you are," said Jared. "Here I am, fallen in the line of duty, wounded in the hour of conflict, and all you can do is slap me in the face."

"Will you knock it off?" Sarah continued with her words of comfort and cheer.

Jared's mouth was dry, but he managed to say, "I think I figured it out!"

"You mean that you have a problem with blood?"

"No! I think I know what the last clue was. ISAM 167. It's First Samuel 16:7!"

"Really?" Sarah said. She actually sounded impressed. At least a little.

Jared recited the verse. "'Man looks at the outward appearance, but the Lord looks at the heart.' What was the last thing the Horseman said to us?"

"Remember the verse," Sarah recalled.

"Right."

"So . . . Dr. Maggini is not what he appears," Sarah concluded.

"Yep," continued Jared. "Dr. Maggini is full of . . . " And they both said it together:

"5317!"

Sarah looked at the bottle in her hand. "So the blood on his forehead was probably this stuff—he was faking it when he told us he got knocked in the head. And since he remembered you got dizzy when you saw blood, he put a puddle of fake blood here to scare you off."

As Sarah figured things out, Jared slowly sat up. He was recovering now. Breathing quite nicely, thank you. *Of course, it would help to have a nice, tall glass of lemonade with a side of warm, homemade chocolate chip cookies,* Jared thought. *You know, to get my blood sugar level up to acceptable medical standards. And maybe a slice of cheesecake with a sweet graham cracker crust and cherry sauce dripping off the sides where it . . .*

"Well, are you just gonna sit there all day?" Sarah asked as sweetly as a drill sergeant with a toothache. "We've got to get that violin! It's our only link to finding Mr. Whittaker!"

"I need to rest for just a minute, all right?" Jared shot back.

"You are such a wimp," Sarah said under her breath.

Her words sliced into him. But they also confirmed something he'd been thinking for quite a while. The more he'd thought about it, the more it made sense. He got up from the monster chair that had swallowed him.

"I'm going home," he said.

"What?!"

"Maybe I *am* a wimp," Jared said, "but I'm not stupid."

"What are you talking about?" Sarah asked.

"Stop and think about it, Sarah. What are we *doing* here? We're following a guy who's already kidnapped Mr. Whittaker. So what's this guy gonna do to *us?*"

Sarah didn't say anything. Maybe his point had hit home.

"Okay," Jared continued. "To be honest, this has been real fun and all, but now it's getting dangerous. Like *you and me* are gonna stop this Maggini guy? I don't think so." He paused. "C'mon, Sarah," he said, "it's time to call it quits and let the pros take it from here."

"So I guess I'm right," Sarah said. "You *are* a wimp." She turned her back to him. "Go home if you want. I'm gonna find Mr. Whittaker *myself.*"

Sarah pointed her flashlight at the gaping, black hole in the wall. With her chin held high, she walked straight toward the tunnel. And disappeared into it.

Jared sighed and shook his head. Next step, he needed to call the police—for Sarah's sake as well as Mr. Whittaker's. He headed for the stairway with new vigor. Then he stopped.

What was that noise he'd just heard? It sounded like someone clearing her throat!

"Jared?"

He turned around. Sarah stood at the tunnel entrance. "I . . . I hate tunnels. Can you help me?"

Jared looked down at the floor and sighed. "No," he said quietly.

"Just help me find the violin. That's all. C'mon. For Mr. Whittaker."

Sarah held out the flashlight.

Jared stepped forward . . . and took it.

He pointed the flashlight beam toward the hole in the wall. Under his breath, Jared prayed, *God, I need You.* He tried to keep the beam steady, to stop it from shaking so much. And he tried not to breathe so loudly. Carefully, carefully, he stepped forward.

"Jared?" Sarah whispered.

"Yeah?" whispered Jared back.

"I'm sorry I called you a wimp."

Jared sighed. "It's okay. And . . . I'm sorry I thought you were stupid."

There was a pause.

"*You* thought *I* was stupid?" Sarah said.

"Look, I *said* I was sorry."

"You sure are," said Sarah, her voice louder than it should have been.

"All right," said Jared. "We can stay here and fight, or we can go in that tunnel together. What's it gonna be?"

"Okay, okay."

Jared took a step forward—and they were inside. Sarah followed closely. The tunnel was humid. The dank walls felt close, and it smelled like his grandma's cellar.

It was deathly quiet. But inwardly, Jared was a mass of questions. *What are we gonna find? What if we run into Dr. Maggini? What if we run into the Hooded Horseman? Will we ever find the violin? Will we ever find Mr. Whittaker?*

Whoa! His flashlight shone on a metal bucket on the floor right next to the wall. It had a few rocks inside. *Good thing I saw that before I slammed into it.*

KRRRRACK!

The silence they had worked so hard to keep was now broken. Jared and Sarah stood absolutely still. The sound had come from deep inside the unseen passageway ahead. They looked at each other. It sounded like a piece of wood cracking. *But what could it be?*

Jared clicked off his flashlight so they wouldn't be spotted. From the depths of the tunnel another light beam now probed the walls. Sarah gasped. She pulled Jared backward. Jared backed up with her—CLANG! Sarah hit the bucket!

"Who's there?!" A voice echoed from deep in the tunnel. The voice of Dr. Maggini!

The flashlight beam got brighter as it came closer. Jared held his breath.

"I said, who's there?!" he demanded.

The light beam from the tunnel flashed back and forth, searching, probing like a predator on the prowl.

"I'm warning you. I've got a bomb. One more step inside this tunnel and I'm setting this thing off!"

Jared looked at Sarah. *What now?* They heard some

tools or something being scooped up. Then footsteps running away, farther into the tunnel.

After a moment, silence.

Jared took a few steps forward as he peered down the tunnel with his flashlight.

"What about the bomb?" Sarah whispered.

Jared replied with a number. "5317."

"Right," said Sarah.

Gingerly, Jared stepped forward. He *hoped* the part about the bomb was a lie. Sarah fell in behind Jared, and they plunged deeper into the dank darkness. The tunnel twisted slightly back and forth, so it was hard to see very far ahead. Jared tried not to think about what was around the next bend.

After a hundred paces or so, Jared's flashlight beam caught something on the ground up ahead: an object with graceful lines, a dark cherry-brown finish, and a curving scroll at the top. *The violin! The Amati violin!*

arah forgot any fear as she raced forward with Jared. The flashlight beam bounced up and down with their steps. When they arrived, Jared pointed the light down.

And there was the violin. Sarah felt her heart drop. The neck was broken as if someone had purposefully cracked it from the body. The left carved hole on the front was peeled back, with splinters of wood sticking up.

"This is awful," she whispered as she knelt down.

"But why would he do this?" Jared wondered aloud. "It's worth at least a couple million bucks. This doesn't make sense!"

"I know."

She gingerly picked up the violin. "Help me."

Jared helped her scoop under the instrument, and she stood up with the violin in her arms. It felt like she was holding some rare, exotic animal that was broken and dying.

Meanwhile, Jared paced the tunnel. "When we were in the Imagination Station, the Horseman said Mr. Whittaker was kidnapped, right?"

"Right."

"I'm not sure if I've got this all figured out yet," said Jared, "but it's looking more and more like Dr. Maggini is the one who kidnapped him."

"Yep, that makes sense," said Sarah.

"Which means—as stupid as I think this is . . . "

"We've got to follow Dr. Maggini!"

"Right."

"C'mon, Sarah," Jared motioned for her to follow. "For Mr. Whittaker!"

Sarah smiled. That was what she had been thinking all along.

As they ran, Sarah heard a rhythmic jangling in Jared's pocket—he was still carrying Mr. Whittaker's keys. A radical idea crossed her mind.

Jared and Sarah emerged from the tunnel into the night air. They were in the woods behind Whit's End. Sarah thought she heard a car trunk open. The sound came from the little parking lot behind Whit's End. She and Jared ran toward the sound.

Two cars were in the small gravel lot—one was Mr.

Whittaker's. The other was a gray car that Sarah didn't recognize. Its trunk was gaping open like the jaws of a great shark. Jared ducked behind a tree to watch. Sarah joined him.

Dr. Maggini emerged from the shadows, carrying what looked like a huge sack on his back. He stumbled. *That sack looks big enough to hold a person,* Sarah thought. Then she realized, *Mr. Whittaker is in that sack!*

She looked over at Jared. His mouth was wide open. The car trunk slammed shut.

Don Cortado woke up. He winced in pain. The ropes around his wrists were tied so tightly to the chair that his fingers were numb. His legs—strapped to the chair's legs—didn't feel much better. Still he managed somehow to rock and scoot over to the window, just in time to see a gray car squeal around the corner and take off, most likely heading toward the airport.

Trying not to tip over the chair, he wiggled his way as best he could toward the desk. *Whit always kept a neat desk,* he remembered.

Cortado could barely feel his fingers, but he was close enough to the desk to reach the phone cord running down the side. He pulled on it with his thumb and index finger. The phone scooted across the desk . . . toward the edge . . . closer, and . . . BAM! It landed on the floor. The receiver separated from the base on impact. He could hear the dial tone.

Now came the tricky part: determining how to get down on the floor without breaking any important body parts. He rocked the chair back and forth . . . back and . . . SLAM! He collided with the floor, hitting his right shoulder with a painful blow. There was no time to analyze the injury. His numb fingers reached out—and dialed.

Sarah and Jared panted, out of breath, as they stood in the little parking lot beside Mr. Whittaker's car. Sarah figured Jared wanted to get a better view of the speeding getaway car from here. But she had other plans.

"Let's go after him," Sarah said.

"What do you mean?"

"By the time we call the police and explain everything, they'll be long gone."

"You want to *run* after the guy?" asked Jared.

"No. *Drive.*"

"Are you nuts?"

"Maybe so. You still have Mr. Whittaker's keys, don't you?"

"Did I mention you were nuts?" Jared said.

"Look," Sarah continued. "We don't know if Mr. Whittaker is dead or alive. But if he's still alive, we've got to go after him. Who knows what Dr. Maggini will do to him? C'mon! We're losing time just standing here talking!"

Jared paused a second. Then he whipped out the keys, opened the car door, and jumped in the driver's seat.

"You're pretty good at the Demolition Derby Race Car game, aren't you?" asked Sarah as she got in her side.

"Yeah," said Jared, trying to adjust the driver's seat.

"Okay, then. It shouldn't be *too* much different."

"Oh no!"

The seat was set for Mr. Whittaker—who was not only an adult, but a very full-sized version. Jared was too short for the pedals. He tried to adjust the seat. Stuck.

Sarah intervened. "All right, I'll get the gas and brake. You steer." She flopped on the floorboard, ready to go, even though she couldn't see anything. She looked up at Jared—key in his hand, reaching for the ignition. He was almost too shaky to put the key in place.

"This is totally ridiculous," he said.

"We don't have much of a choice, do we?"

"Forget what I said. *You* are totally ridiculous!"

"Are we gonna fight or work together?" Sarah asked.

Jared didn't say anything.

"You can do it," she encouraged.

Jared twisted the ignition. The engine turned. Sarah pushed on the gas pedal.

Va-RRROOOOOOOOOOOOM!

Sarah watched as Jared put the car in gear. She felt the transmission clunk into place.

"Gas!" Jared shouted.

Sarah slammed down the gas pedal.

She heard the tires squeal, kick up some gravel . . . and off they went, one to steer, one to start and stop.

"Yes?" Klaushack growled into the phone.

The wheels of the jet touched the asphalt.

"Do you have Whittaker?"

The blue lights of the runway zipped past the window.

"Alive?"

The engines reversed to slow the screaming plane.

"Good. Very good."

Jared couldn't believe what he was doing. But there was no time to think.

"Brake!" Jared yelled as coolly as he could. Sarah pushed on the brake pedal just as Jared came up behind a parked pickup truck on the street. "Gas!" He spun the steering wheel and veered around the truck. His stomach veered along with it.

"I just thought about something," Sarah remarked from the floorboard as Jared frantically maneuvered through the night traffic.

"Gas!" Jared yelled.

Whoa! Brake lights ahead!

"Brake—Brake! Whoa!"

Jared swung to the left lane and passed a pickup truck, almost clipping the rear bumper. "Yikes!"

"Are you listening to me?" Sarah asked.

"Uh, sure!"

"See, everything relates to the verse! 'Man looks at the outward appearance, but God looks at the heart.' Don't you see it?"

It was probably good *Sarah* couldn't "see it" as they took a chaotic path down the highway.

"Gas!" Jared called out, trying to catch up to an invisible car that was probably long gone anyway.

Sarah pushed on the gas as she went on. "Everything we saw wasn't what it looked like. Dr. Maggini *looked like* a professor, but turned out to be a bad guy. The Hooded Horseman *looked like* he was a thief, but turned out to be a good guy—maybe. And now I'm wondering about the violin . . ."

I'm wondering if we'll make it through this night alive, thought Jared. "Brake! Brake!" he yelled.

They slowed to a jerky stop at a red light.

The stupidity of all this hit him. *What if the police pull me over? They'd probably bar me from ever having a driver's license in my entire life! What if I wreck? What if Sarah got hurt? What if I ran into somebody else, and* they *got hurt? But then again, Mr. Whittaker's life could be in danger.*

Something interrupted his thoughts. Jared squinted. About a mile ahead was a large hill. A gray car crested the top before disappearing on the other side. The light turned green. Jared swallowed the lump in his throat and yelled, "Gas!"

The car jerked forward as Sarah continued. "So the violin could be a fake, for all we know. Or else . . . we're looking at the outside, but the important part is what's on the inside. I mean, look at how the violin was smashed—as if there was something valuable inside."

"Whoa! Brake! Brake!" Jared called out in the calmest panic he could muster. Wide-eyed, white-faced, and white-knuckled, he tried to catch his breath as he stared at the back of a semi-truck that seemed like mere inches away.

"Gas!" Jared steered around the truck.

"After all," Sarah continued, "why would anyone want to destroy a violin in the first place? But what's the valuable thing that was inside?"

Jared followed the gray car into the entrance marked "Odyssey Municipal Airport." The car took a little side road and stopped at a gate with barbed wire at the top. A red-and-white sign announced "NO ENTRANCE. *Security Clearance Required.*" Jared watched Dr. Maggini stick his hand out the window and place it on a yellow machine beside the car. *Obviously, some kind of handprint identification system.* A green bulb lit up above the machine. The gate slid to the left.

"Gas! Gas!" Jared yelled.

Sarah hit the gas. "On the other hand, what about the Horseman?"

Jared steered as best he could as the gray car zoomed forward. But now the gate was closing!

"More gas!" Jared bellowed. Sarah pushed even more on the pedal. VA-ROOOOOOOM!

The car headed straight for the closing gate! Jared shut his eyes.

"You know," Sarah said, "I kinda wonder what his role is in all of this."

"AAAAAAAAAAAAHHHH!"

"What's wrong with you?" Sarah asked from down below. Jared opened his eyes again. He checked the rear-view mirror just as the gate closed behind him!

"Um, wrong?" Jared replied, "What could be wrong?" He let out a nervous chuckle.

The gray car suddenly rocketed forward and to the right, hugging the corner of an airplane hangar as it arced around. *He must've spotted us,* thought Jared. He steered to the right.

There were hangars on each side of him now, but the gray car was gone.

"Coast!" Jared called out.

Sarah let go of the pedals. The car coasted forward as Jared looked left and right between buildings. *Aha!*

"Brake!"

The car stopped. *Aha!* Jared spotted Dr. Maggini running up the steps into a jet. The door on the jet closed, and the plane pulled forward. *Now what?*

Jared figured if he zoomed out in front of the plane now, it would just steer around him. *Maybe if we can get* behind *the plane and stop it somehow. But we need to follow it without being seen.*

Working with Sarah, Jared backed up and made a big

97

U-turn around the hangars, then headed back to the taxiway where he had seen the plane. At least, he *thought* it was the same taxiway. He looked both ways, but there was no plane! He drove a little farther ahead. That's when things got confusing. Taxiways and runways crisscrossed each other in the night. *Just great. Maybe the jet already took off.* But he would've heard it, wouldn't he?

Strange. He could now hear the sound of a jet approaching, but there wasn't one anywhere in sight—until he checked his rearview mirror, that is. There was the jet, getting steadily larger and larger!

"What's going on up there?" Sarah asked.

"You don't want to know." Jared prayed, "Dear God . . . HELP!"

"Now I'm worried," said Sarah. "You usually wait until you're in trouble to pray."

Jared ignored that. Even though the car was moving forward, the jet was now bearing down on them as it filled the rearview mirror. An idea popped into his head.

"Brake, brake!"

Sarah hit the brakes. The car stopped quickly. It looked like the jet was trying to brake, but it was too late. Even though the jet wasn't going very fast, it would be quite an impact.

"Hang on!" Jared yelled as the plane came closer and closer.

POW! KRRRRRRRUNCH!

The jet rammed the back of the car with a jolt and a loud crash of metal. Both vehicles came to a halt on the runway. Sirens wailed in the distance.

"What was *that?*" Sarah asked, rubbing her head. The impact had knocked her against the floorboard.

Jared didn't respond. He looked out of the smashed rear window. The jet door was already unfolded. *What?* He looked toward the hangars just as Dr. Maggini darted into one. A moment later, the gray car squealed out of the hangar. Jared glanced to his left. *The exit gate!*

"Gas! Gas!" yelled Jared.

"Are you sure?"

"Gas, Sarah!"

Sarah hit the gas. The front wheels spun on the pavement, then took hold as Jared steered the car—turning and aiming straight for the exit.

"Hold on tight, Sarah!"

"What?"

"BRAKE HARD!"

The car slid sideways and slammed against the fence—straddling the exit gate. Dr. Maggini slammed on his brakes. But it was too late.

SKREEEEEEEK! KRRRRRUNCHSHHHHH! KSSSSSSSSSH!

It was an awful sound, a mixture of crunching metal and crashing glass. The impact jostled Jared and Sarah around. But the gray car was out of commission. *Mission accomplished. Well, almost.* The twisted exit gate squeaked and squealed as it wobbled and slid open.

Dr. Maggini jumped out of the car and ran toward the gate. Two security officers burst through a door in the side of the passenger terminal. They closed in on the fleeing suspect. Dr. Maggini looked over his shoulder. The two officers tackled him to the ground.

Sarah got up from the floor. "Okay, Jared, what is going—" She gasped. There were police cars and big black cars with flashing red and blue lights all around, a smashed-up gray car beside them, and a disabled jet behind them.

Sarah looked at Jared. "Next time, *I* drive," she said.

Jared jumped out and ran to the car beside them. *What is he doing now?* thought Sarah. *But wait. That's the same car we saw at Whit's End!*

Instantly, she knew what was happening. She hopped out the driver's side and joined Jared at the back of the gray car. A dull thumping noise came from the trunk.

"Hold on, Mr. Whittaker!" Sarah shouted.

Jared grabbed the car keys from the ignition and opened the trunk. The lid opened to reveal Mr. Whittaker, bound with ropes and a gag over his mouth. He looked pale, but once he saw Jared and Sarah, his eyes lit up. Sarah untied Mr. Whittaker's gag as Jared untied the other ropes.

Mr. Whittaker burst out, "Jared! Sarah! I'm so glad you two are all right!" Jared and Sarah helped him out of the trunk. He stood up. Sarah noticed his legs were a bit wobbly from being bound for so long. But Mr. Whittaker still managed to give them both a hearty hug. She grinned.

Then Sarah noticed Mr. Whittaker's eyes narrowing. She turned to see four police officers emerge from the jet, escorting a big man with curly gray hair and bushy eyebrows.

"Klaushack!" Mr. Whittaker said to himself. "Well, I'll be!"

The big man turned in their direction. He shouted across the runway. "So, Whittaker, you finally did it!" He held up his handcuffs. "Are you proud of yourself?"

"It wasn't me, Klaushack!" Mr. Whittaker shouted back. "This time I had some help!"

Mr. Whittaker smiled at Jared and Sarah and said quietly, " . . . from some good friends."

"You're right, Whit!"

I've heard that voice before, Sarah thought. *I've heard that accent!*

Mr. Whittaker gasped.

A tall man stepped out of the shadows—a tan-skinned man with a thin black mustache. Sarah's eyes grew wide. *The Hooded Horseman!*

He looked striking in his black suit and tie. Mr. Whittaker looked shocked. "Don!" he cried. And the two men hugged as if they were long-lost friends. Sarah figured that's exactly what they were.

Sarah and Jared sat in the back of a speeding police cruiser. The radio spouted some kind of police code as the siren screamed through the night. The flashing red and blue lights lit up houses on either side of them.

The cruiser pulled up at Whit's End, which was ablaze in white light. Two news vans stood sentry out front, their microwave antennae probing the night sky. Reporters talked into microphones and interviewed people on the front lawn.

Sarah looked closer. They were interviewing her parents!

"Mom, Dad!" Sarah ran into their arms, and the family was reunited on the eleven o'clock news.

When Jared's parents saw him, they gave him a huge hug. His mom had mascara streaks down her face.

The police officer who had brought Jared and Sarah gently reminded them that they were needed inside for some questions. Sarah took a deep breath.

Jared sat down in Mr. Whittaker's office along-side Sarah. They had an important government function to fulfill. Yes, Agent 3XQ was back in action. Although this time, it was for real!

Mr. Whittaker sat down in the leather chair behind his desk. His friend, the Hooded Horseman—a.k.a. ("also known as" in spy-speak) Don Cortado—sat in a chair beside him.

Across the room sat two government guys, dressed in dark suits, armed with recording devices and electronic notepads. It was all part of the "O.D.S." or "Official Debrief Session."

"Well," said Mr. Whittaker with a chuckle. "This is a bit cozy, but isn't it a wonderful way to get to know each other better?" The government guys didn't crack a smile. They simply went back to their electronic notepads.

Jared guessed they wrote down, "humor needs work."

The one with red hair and a crew cut went by the name of "Dave" (although Jared was certain that wasn't his real name) and spoke with robust authority. You could tell this guy loved his job.

"May I remind you that everything said at this meeting is strictly confidential. You are prohibited from divulging any information you gain from this meeting or else risk the compromise of national security and/or be found guilty of violating federal law."

Jared was impressed with his speech, especially that "and/or" part, which the man spoke with a professional gusto.

The other man—the muscular, grim-faced one—never said a word. He nodded in an all-knowing way now and then, scratched his chin, and wrote another note on his electronic pad.

"I suppose it's mostly up to me to tell the *other* side of the story for you," Mr. Cortado said, winking at Mr. Whittaker.

"You may proceed," said "Dave." And so Mr. Cortado "proceeded."

"First off," he said with his slight Hispanic accent, "Dr. Maggini isn't a doctor and isn't a Maggini. His name is Mason Wasatchi, and he's a member of a political crime network based in Switzerland known as Red Scorpion. This group is known as a professional terrorist agency that sells its unique 'services' to clients around the globe.

"Over the past year, the National Security Agency—

the NSA—has successfully infiltrated Red Scorpion in order to get more information on their activities and eventually destroy the organization.

"A week ago, Wasatchi stole a micro-zip disk from the NSA. On that disk was a list of our undercover NSA agents who were working at Red Scorpion. If Red Scorpion got hold of that disk, our agents would die. Nicolas Klaushack, the director of Red Scorpion, personally offered Wasatchi a five-million-dollar 'bonus' for the disk.

"But now the question," Mr. Cortado continued. "How could Wasatchi get this disk to Klaushack in Switzerland? He didn't trust sending the information by any electronic method—and he felt sure he was being followed. How could this list be well guarded without drawing any attention to it?

"He came up with a plan, with some help from a Red Scorpion agent who worked at the Chicago Museum of Music and Culture. Wasatchi's friend knew that the museum was about to loan several precious items to the Swiss National Museum—among them, the precious Amati violin. Keep in mind that the violin—although it was rare—was only worth about half the bonus Wasatchi was getting.

"So, with his friend's help, Wasatchi slipped the disk through the carved hole in the violin. Using tweezers, he carefully glued it to the interior. With a Red Scorpion agent already in place at the Swiss museum, it looked like a foolproof plan.

"Unfortunately for Wasatchi, I was onto him from the start because his 'friend' at the Chicago museum was actually an NSA undercover agent. With the agent's help, I got the violin. But before I could thoroughly look it over, Wasatchi got wind of what was happening. Somebody had blown my cover. Now Wasatchi was on *my* tail. There was no time to find and retrieve the disk.

"At this point, I didn't trust anyone. I had my hands on a ticking bomb. The museum was after the violin, because it was precious. Wasatchi wanted the violin because Klaushack would pay him millions of dollars for it, and Klaushack wanted the violin because the disk would help him 'clean house' at Red Scorpion.

"That's when I came to Odyssey and the one person I knew I could trust—my old NSA buddy, John Whittaker."

"Aha!" said Jared.

Sarah glared at Jared, and Dave coolly repeated his warning: "May I remind you that everything said at this meeting is strictly confidential. You are prohibited from divulging any information you gain from this meeting or else risk the compromise of national security and/or be found guilty of violating federal law."

Wow, Jared thought. *This guy is like one of those purple teddy bears where you push his belly button and he says the same thing over and over again.* But he didn't want to tell Dave that.

Mr. Cortado turned to Jared and Sarah. "Wasatchi

was also part of the NSA at one time—before he defected."

"So that's why you called him a traitor!" said Sarah.

"It fits," said Mr. Cortado. "See, Whit and I developed an early prototype of the Imagination Station. When Whit left the NSA, Wasatchi took his place. Once he learned virtual technology, he disappeared—taking NSA's secrets with him.

"Wasatchi shared this technology with Klaushack—a major drug dealer. The NSA asked Whit to come back to help us use the technology against Klaushack. It worked, and we broke up Klaushack's drug network. All the major players were caught and sentenced to prison, except for Klaushack and Wasatchi. That's when Klaushack turned from dealing in drugs to dealing in terror. You see—"

Dave interjected. "Let's get back to the story at hand, Mr. Cortado."

"Oh," said Mr. Cortado. "Yes. Of course . . . "

He went on. "So as soon as I got to Odyssey, I tracked down Whit. But Wasatchi was close behind me. To avoid him, I came in through the window in the Bible Room. But I couldn't find you," he said, looking at Mr. Whittaker.

"I was in the Kids' Radio Studio at the time," explained Mr. Whittaker.

"I couldn't hear you anywhere, either."

"Because it's soundproof," Mr. Whittaker said.

"Ah, of course. Well, I made my way to the basement

and the secret tunnel—the one you showed me when I was here last time. I hid the violin there. As I came back upstairs, I looked out the window and spotted Wasatchi circling the building in his car. I knew I was in danger.

"I wanted to leave Whit certain clues to the violin, in case anything happened to me. On an earlier visit, Whit had shown me the latest version of the Imagination Station—the one right here at Whit's End. That gave me an idea. I created my own Imagination Station adventure. I plugged in what I knew about 1600s Italy and combined it with an existing program about Odyssey history. Then I planted clues only *you* would be able to figure out, Whit—clues that would lead you to the violin."

"So the Hooded Horseman . . . " began Mr. Whittaker.

"Was a virtual replica of me," finished Mr. Cortado, "designed to help lead you to the clues. As the Horseman, I kept myself hidden under the cloak, just in case Wasatchi got into the program. I didn't want him to recognize me."

"Unfortunately, before I could finish programming the escape portals, Wasatchi came in through the window behind me. He sprayed me with Comatosin—"

Dave interrupted. "Red Scorpion's own knock-out compound."

"Right," Mr. Cortado replied.

Dave wrote it down on his pad as Mr. Cortado continued.

"That's when Wasatchi tied me up and dragged me here to your office."

Mr. Whittaker nodded. "That must be about the time I came upstairs. It looked like someone had been fooling with the Imagination Station, so I went to check it out. When I got locked inside, the kids followed me—and so did Wasatchi. He must've been hiding in the Control Room. That's the only other way to enter the the adventure besides the Imagination Station itself."

"And that's when Wasatchi became 'Dr. Maggini,'" Mr. Cortado noted.

"I see now," said Mr. Whittaker. "He wanted me to figure out the clues for him, so he could find the *real* violin."

"Exactly."

"So *that's* what happened to our horse." Mr. Whittaker put it together. "When Wasatchi got enough clues, he slipped some Comatosin to the horse as a diversion, so he could get to the town alone."

"Only problem was," said Mr. Cortado, "Wasatchi never figured on the kids being part of the equation— and those kids became his downfall."

Jared sat up straighter in his chair, with the humble knowledge that his superior detective skills had saved the day. He glanced over at Sarah, who just looked relieved.

Mr. Whittaker scratched his chin. "Jared mentioned something about the Bible verse, First Samuel 16:7. How did you think of using that?" he asked.

"It was posted in the Bible Room," replied Mr. Cortado. "Ah!"

Dave stabbed his electronic pen in the air as he summarized. "So we've got Cortado unconscious in the office. Whittaker and the two kids are trapped in the Imagination Station. And Wasatchi joins them."

"That's correct," replied Mr. Whittaker. "Toward the end of the adventure, I went into a livery stable and discovered a portal out of the Imagination Station. But before I could go back and tell the kids about it, Wasatchi—also known as Dr. Maggini—sprayed me with Comatosin.

"Wasatchi already had all the clues he wanted, so I suppose he went back to disable the Imagination Station with Jared and Sarah inside. That way, no one else could trail him."

Mr. Cortado picked it up from there. "I was still bound to this chair here," Don said, tapping the armrest. "But I could see Wasatchi take off in his car toward the airport. I managed to work my way over to the phone and call for help to take me to the airport.

"And that's where—thanks to Jared and Sarah—Wasatchi was arrested, along with Nicolas Klaushack, the executive director of Red Scorpion. Some kind of night, huh?"

Jared sat there in his chair, eyes wide, mouth hanging open.

Sarah was asleep.

t's good to be back at Whit's End again, thought Sarah. It was six o'clock on a Saturday night.

The place was packed with kids everywhere . . . slurping sodas at the Soda Shop, exploring the Bible Room upstairs, re-creating historic train wrecks in the Train Room.

And just today, the Imagination Station was up and running again, finally! The line of kids—waiting to take their own adventures—stretched all the way into the hall. Yep, it was a normal day, as far as normal goes in the town of Odyssey.

Jared sat beside Sarah at the soda counter as he picked over the remains of a Raspberry Ripple. *He's probably looking for digestible spy cameras in the raspberry seeds,* thought Sarah.

A horn honked outside.

"That's him!" cried Sarah. "C'mon, Jared!" She jumped down off the stool.

"Wait, Sarah," Jared said, holding up a spoon. "Does this raspberry seed look rather . . . *unusual* to you?"

Sure enough, everything *was* back to normal.

Sarah rolled her eyes.

"Why do you always do that?" Jared asked. "You always roll your eyes like that!"

"That's because you are such a . . . a . . . *boy!* Now will you put down that spoon? Mr. Whittaker is waiting for us!" The horn honked again.

"Wow, new car?" asked Jared as he and Sarah shut the car doors and buckled their seat belts.

"No," Mr. Whittaker replied. "Just a rental till I get mine out of the shop."

"Oh," said Jared. Sarah thought she heard a little pain in his voice.

"So today was your last day, then?" asked Mr. Whittaker as he pointed the car toward Connellsville.

"Yes, sir," replied Sarah. "And I'm so glad it's over." She rubbed her shoulder. It was still sore from picking up litter around Olde Gate Road earlier that day. She and Jared were "volunteers" for the Keep Odyssey Beautiful campaign. Well, not really *volunteers*. For driving a car without a license, the county judge had sentenced them both to six months of

113

weekend community service. It could have been worse. But the judge took into consideration how much the kids had helped authorities track down a bad guy and rescue Mr. Whittaker.

A ball of sun hung low on the horizon and lit up the yellow and orange leaves along the road to Connellsville. Sarah looked forward to the evening ahead.

Once in town, Mr. Whittaker dropped some coins in the parking meter and led the way to the old Connellsville Concert Hall.

"Come in, come in!" A short, balding man with a neatly trimmed white goatee unlocked the front entrance and swung open the brass and glass doorway. "This is one very exciting evening, sir!" said the man, who looked to be in his seventies.

"Very much so," Mr. Whittaker said. "Louis," he said as he gestured, "this is Jared DeWhite and Sarah Prachett."

Out of nowhere, a camera flash went off.

"Oh! Sorry about that!" Louis apologized as Sarah blinked to regain her eyesight. "That's our publicity person."

A toothy-smiling guy in his twenties waved from behind his camera.

Louis turned to Sarah and Jared. "So these are the heroes!"

Jared beamed and Sarah smiled sheepishly as Mr. Whittaker continued with the introductions. "Jared and Sarah, this is Louis Longino, the concertmaster for the Connellsville Symphony Orchestra. He's the one who assists the conductor and leads the first violin section."

"Nice to meet you," said Jared, with a firm handshake.

"Good to meet you, Mr. Longino," Sarah said.

Mr. Longino's blue eyes sparkled with enthusiasm. "Well, let's not wait any longer! Come with me!"

Mr. Whittaker, Jared, and Sarah followed the aging concertmaster through the marble foyer into the main auditorium. The ceiling soared high above them, chandeliers hung down, and a huge, rich red-velvet curtain with ornate gold embroidery covered the stage. Brass angels holding lamps adorned the exits. Sarah drew a deep breath, taking it all in. Then she coughed. It was a bit musty. Still, it was a grand old place.

Mr. Longino led them to a room backstage, lined with music stands and old wooden chairs. "You'll get to hear this at tonight's concert, of course, but I wanted to give you three a 'sneak preview.'"

Taking a key from his pocket, Mr. Longino reached up to a cabinet to unlock it. Gingerly, he pulled a black violin case from the shelf.

Mr. Whittaker had donated the money to have the Amati restored through his Universal Press Foundation. The restoration was meticulous, demanding, and complicated work, but Mr. Whittaker said it was a worthy investment in history. And now, six months later,

Sarah and Jared were about to see and hear the violin in its old glory, before it was returned "home" to the Chicago Museum of Music and Culture.

Mr. Longino clicked open the latches. Sarah could almost hear the music as the lid fell back to reveal . . . the Amati violin! She gasped. It was beautiful! The lights in the ceiling reflected in its shiny lacquered finish and its deep reddish-brown wood.

"Ah, but wait until you *hear!*" Mr. Longino said as he lifted the old instrument out of the case as carefully as if he were taking a sleeping baby from its crib. He placed the violin on his shoulder, set his bow across the strings . . . and the 338-year-old violin came to life again. Its voice filled the room with a sweet and noble presence. Mr. Longino closed his eyes, and the music soared in a melody that was both sad and beautiful.

Mr. Whittaker smiled. Sarah stood perfectly still and drank in the music. When it came to the last, long note, Jared uttered his own musical accolade. "Pretty cool," he said. Sarah shook her head. *Jared. Hopeless.*

One hour later, Sarah took her seat in an empty red-velvet chair beside her mom and dad. Next to Sarah was Jared, then his parents, then Mr. Whittaker and Mr. Cortado. All front row seats. All honored guests. Sarah looked over her shoulder at still *more* people arriving at the already packed building. Latecomers. And it *was* late. The concert should have started twenty minutes ago. But the red curtain stood at attention and didn't move. There was a murmur in the house as the audience tried to fill the time with conversation.

"I wonder what's taking so long," said Sarah.

"I don't know. You have any Cheese Doodles on you?" asked Jared.

"This is a concert hall, not a football stadium," Sarah chided. *Boys,* she thought. *Cultural pygmies.*

Still, she had to admit her new appreciation for this particular pygmy. Tonight was the end of a wild adventure, and Jared had been an important part of it. Sure, it would be hard to obey those government security rules and keep their exciting escapade to themselves. But she knew they would never forget what they had learned about courage and teamwork—and not judging each other by outward appearances.

Mr. Whittaker leaned over to Sarah and Jared. "You know, I've got an idea for the next Kids' Radio production."

Sarah was intrigued. Her last production aired about a month after their violin adventure. "Daisy Mae, the Ugly Flower" was a pithy radio drama that got wonderful reviews from her mom and most of Sarah's friends at school. Jared had received the most praise for his rendition of Sam the Arrogant Bumblebee.

Mr. Whittaker continued. "This time, I'd like both of you to work on it together." It wasn't that long ago that Sarah would have never *considered* working with Jared.

"I'd like you to base it on First Corinthians 12:21,"

said Mr. Whittaker. "Listen to this," he said as he pulled a little black Bible from his pocket and adjusted his glasses to read the small print. "The eye cannot say to the hand, 'I don't need you!' And the head cannot say to the feet, 'I don't need you!'"

Mr. Whittaker said, "Fact is, God designed us so we all need each other."

"Wait," Jared said, "You want us to base a radio drama on *that?*"

"If anybody can do it, I know you two can," said Mr. Whittaker, a twinkle in his eye.

"Pssst! Pssst!"

Sarah glanced up. In the exit on the right was Mr. Longino, waving his hand, trying to get their attention. Mr. Whittaker, Jared, and Sarah quickly made their way to the exit where Mr. Longino was standing. He pulled them all aside. "We need your help!" he whispered.

"What's wrong?" Mr. Whittaker asked.

The concertmaster looked all around to make sure no one was listening. Then he delivered the news. "Our *tuba* is missing! We think someone might have stolen it!"

Sarah and Jared turned to each other in perfect unison. "Oh *nooooo!*"

Dedication

This book is dedicated to God, who inspires me to "go for it," and to my Mom, who believed in me before anybody else did.

Thanks to Robin Crouch, my very first editor and coach, who encouraged me and pushed me just enough. To John Duckworth—I'm honored that such a talented guy cared enough to spend so much time investing in this project. I also appreciate Jenny Baumgartner, Laura Minchew, Dee Ann Grand, and Heather Hardison for their editorial help. And thank you to Aunt Cissy, whose dusty violin in the attic inspired a book. To Christopher, Robert, and Melissa—it's the greatest privilege in the world to call you kids my own.

Most of all, thanks to Karen, my love and companion in this exciting real-life adventure, who put up with my late nights as I hammered away at my first book. Because of you, I am blessed way beyond what I deserve.

Welcome to the
Adventures in Odyssey® Family!

We certainly hope you've enjoyed this book. Did your parents or a friend give it to you? Did you see it at the bookstore? Whatever the case, we're thrilled you're making Adventures in Odyssey a part of your day!

If you're like most kids we know, you can't get enough of Adventures in Odyssey, right? Good news! You can also find your favorite AIO characters in:

- Amazing, one-of-a-kind audio dramas on cassette or CD

- Our action-packed line of videos

- Visit our fun-filled Web site bursting with all sorts of interactive adventures at www.whitsend.org.

- Thrilling family games and other activities

All will help you know God better or perhaps "meet" Him for the first time while you're having fun.

Call your Christian radio station to see when "Adventures in Odyssey" airs. Or check your bookstore for other Adventures in Odyssey videos, audio dramas, and paperbacks in the series. More wonder and excitement are right around the corner!

For more information about Adventures in Odyssey, or if we can be of help to your family, simply write to Focus on the Family, Colorado Springs, CO 80995 or call 1-800-A-FAMILY (1-800-232-6459). Friends in Canada may write Focus on the Family, P.O. Box 9800, Stn. Terminal, Vancouver, B.C. V6B 4G3 or call 1-800-661-9800. Visit our Web site—www.family.org—to learn more about Focus on the Family or to find out if there is an associate office in your country

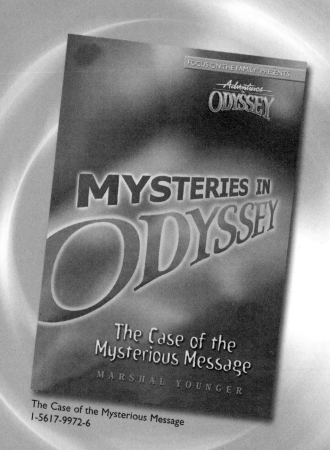